# FINAL YEAR

## MJ MOORES

FINAL YEAR
MJ MOORES

 Love Knot Books

https://loveknotbooks.ca
An imprint of DAOwen Publications

Final Year / MJ Moores
Edited by Douglas Owen and Miles Cruise

Cover art by MMT Productions and Infinite Pathways
ISBN 978-1-928094-45-6
EISBN 978-1-928094-50-0

10 9 8 7 6 5 4 3 2 1

# ACKNOWLEDGMENTS

Diving into the world of romance writing was a decision not easily made. However, once I embraced the fact that all of my writing, no matter the genre, always contained a romantic subplot that either had an HEA (happily ever after) or HFN (happy for now), there was no going back.

While my professional writing journey began with the WCYR (Writers' Community of York Region) and its sisterships, my romantic education flourished when I joined the RWA (Romance Writers of America) and the local Chapter in Toronto (TRW). The seminars, feedback, and support provided helped me gain the confidence I needed to break away from my first love (sci-fi/fantasy) and embrace an unrequited one.

I'd also like to thank my early readers with my two critique groups (The Bradford Writers' Circle and Writers' Ink, Alton Chapter) and my beta readers (Val Tobin, Melissa Barker-Simpson, and Nanci Pattenden). Without their support and advice, Final Year would still be just an idea and some jot notes.

# PANIC

If Beth had known befriending Jeremy's womanizing ass would lead to this, the apology she'd made seven days ago might have been her farewell, too.

Shivering from a brief gust of wind, she zipped up her jacket and continued to pace. The dim light of the underground passageway clashed with the harsh, grey November day breaking through the ivy at the tunnel mouth. The intermittent wail of the campus alarm made Beth's nerves spike. *I should be heading to the stadium with everyone else, just like I told him. Why am I still here?*

Echoes of curiosity jarred with concern as passing voices filtered into the tunnel from the distant crowd beyond the treeline.

*I'm not supposed to be here.*

*You can't ignore what you saw. If anything happens to him between the tunnel and the stadium, you've only yourself to blame.*

*But he's a sweet talker. Used to getting his way—*

"Gah!" She pressed her fists to her forehead fighting

against common sense, logic, the need to follow the rules and still do what's right. The war between her brain and her gut waged on as the scent of the dank earth and moist concrete clung to the hairs at the back of her nose. Beth drew a deep breath through her mouth to avoid the scent of decay.

A pebble clattered from the depths of the darkened tunnel. She froze. Her heart raced–*Run! Leave. Follow the crowd. That could be anyone.* She wanted to obey, but couldn't. Beth barely knew the guy but something–

Footsteps. Foot *drags*. A stuttered stumble and a familiar curse echoed from down the tunnel.

"Jeremy?" Elspeth breathed.

The drip from some distant pipe echoed.

"Elle? You stayed?" He sucked air in between his teeth.

She gave a grim smile at Jeremy's nickname for her, then breached the darkness of the deeper tunnel, dragging her frantic heart back into the abyss. *Relax already. It's probably a false alarm. Precautionary evacuation.* The light in this section burned out, and lack of maintenance meant it would stay that way. The imposing darkness had nothing to do with someone threatening the campus.

In the gloom, she found Jeremy hunched over, leaning heavily against the wall. One hand cradled his head, the other gripped the concrete with pale knuckles. The whiteness of them made her skin crawl, or was it the damp air? She touched his arm.

"What's wrong?"

"Lack of insulin – catching up to me. Making me nauseated. Weak." He drew in a heavy breath.

"We have to get to the stadium. I'm sure they'll have medics there–"

"No."

"What?"

"No. Just get me to the pharmacy. I need my medicine."

"It wasn't in your room?"

He pushed himself from the wall and stumbled forward. His knees gave out. *Shit! He's not acting.*

"Okay! Just give me a minute." Beth surveyed the situation. He'd forgotten his coat and the wind would pierce his sweater in no time. She liked oversized jackets, but his shoulders were twice a broad as hers. *Still...* Beth unzipped her coat and pulled her right arm from her sleeve before kneeling down beside Jeremy. Loose gravel bit into her knees. She couldn't see him well, but the droop of his neck and outline of his parted lips told her she'd made the right decision. Six days ago, Beth had been mistaken and she couldn't afford a repeat of that ignorance. "Put your arm across my back and grip my left shoulder."

He placed it over the coat.

"*Under* my coat, Jeremy. The temperature has dropped. Wind chill."

He carefully slid his arm across her back. She allowed him to breach her bubble of comfort. The jacket pulled tight and tugged against the strain. A brash flitting of her heart startled Beth, causing her to stiffen. *Get it together, Donaldson! You're barely friends.* She made herself shift closer to his lean torso and turned her head toward him as she draped the open-half of her jacket across his back. The tip of her nose accidently brushed his ear. He startled at the contact. She couldn't help but wonder if the jolt was from her unwanted touch or from the feel of her heart pounding against the side of his chest. *What are you doing? Is this really necessary? Just get him to safety already!*

"Grab the sleeve. Slide it on if you can. Make sure your shoulder's covered." Beth slid her hand across his back, noting the contour of each taut muscle and caught her breath. It had been a long time since she'd been this close to a guy. *Stop it. You're not his type. He's not your type.* She moved her fingers, searching for the best grip to help him up, even as their bodies crushed against each other inside her woefully undersized jacket. His torso expanded and contracted as she felt him force slow, deep breaths. Shifting her arm across his spine, Beth settled her hand just under his ribcage.

"Ready? Now."

Grunting and gasping, they struggled to stand. Beth gripped him tighter for stability. The alarm wailed yet another warning, followed by a cop's bull-horn-voice directing the masses to the stadium. Jeremy flinched, sensitive to the harsh sound, as always. The hair on Beth's arms and the back of her neck rose. Her insides tried to flee one way as she forced herself to go in another direction.

They stumbled then walked as one, slowly matching their steps and finding a rhythm – just as they had muddled their way these past weeks chatting over coffee.

Beth used her free arm as a counter-balance. The ivy at the opening to the tunnel wisped against her face. She shut her eyes against the daylight.

"Wait. I can't see yet," she said. He stopped, allowing

her eyes to adjust. She cracked a lid, slowly gaining her bearings. The crisp air bit at her throat as she searched the branching walkway before them. A wall of bushes blocked all but the top of nearby stores.

"Where's your pharmacy?" Beth asked, squinting. The noise of the evacuation hit her full-force now they were outside, but no one walked on this side of the hedge.

"Other side of the bushes," he said.

"Have you come this way before?" she asked.

"Yes."

"We're surrounded by nine-foot hedges. Which way?" She turned them as she looked left and right.

He vaguely waved his hand. "Through. It thins a bit to the right, I believe."

Beth moved them closer. Surprisingly, there was a break in the trunks covered by drooping branches.

"How on earth did you find this spot?"

"I've had a lot of time on campus to discover the best routes to and from certain places. This was a happy accident in my second year."

"Something tells me this isn't the first time you've stumbled over here with a girl."

He smirked. She glanced at his loose, shaggy, blond curls, and ice-grey eyes before shaking her head. *Leave him. Just leave him. He won't care about you once he's got his meds. You're only a tool, Beth. Yeah, a real tool.* But she couldn't leave, and not just because she felt the quake of his ailing body… From the moment she first saw him, her intuition overruled plain and simple logic.

They pushed through the greenery and emerged on the

local campus road, thick with students and professors heading down the extra-wide path toward the stadium.

Jeremy stumbled over the curb. Beth cursed herself for not warning him, tightened her grip around his waist, and widened her stride to compensate. His fingers dug into her shoulder as he staggered, dragging her farther into the crowd. People swarmed around them, jostling and commenting with disgust.

"Which way?" she asked. He leaned on her, his weight making her stagger.

"Should be just ahead. Shop's in the corner of the plaza."

Beth squinted through the crowd. The excitement ran the gamut from near-running strides on the edge of hysteria to small groups of friends pushing and shoving each other as if they knew this was a false-alarm. She could still see the top of the long building adjacent them, but no store signs. *Too many people.* Beth didn't often travel this way on campus, it always felt so isolated from the main concourse and lecture halls. But not now. She could barely move.

Faceless bodies blocked her view. No one bothered to clue-in that they needed help. Disembodied voices assaulted her ears as she elbowed her way through the throng of students.

"–might be terrorism!" a group of girls shrieked, then whimpered as they passed. Jeremy's body stiffened.

"–the police say *emergency evacuation* but no explanation," a guy tried to make sense of the situation.

Beth pushed them through a small break, but the crowd's comments lingered like an aftershock.

"I thought I saw the police with the Dean. Whatever it is, it's serious."

"–think it's a bomb. What else could it be?"

Jeremy's breath hitched at the comment and he coughed, his whole body shuddering.

The alarm wailed. Both of them jumped. Then the voice of the bull-horn cop carried above everyone. Jeremy slammed his free hand over an ear, bashing his head against Beth's to cover the other ear.

"Oww. Jer–"

"Keep calm but keep moving. This is an emergency evacuation. Keep calm but keep moving. Head to the stadium."

Beth glanced along the road, following the weave of bodies down the hill to the safe-zone.

*We have to get out of here.*

*No. You promised you'd help him to the pharmacy.*

A bulky guy in a red York U jersey cut them off. Beth nearly rebounded off his bicep; his cologne reeked of musk and sweat. Coughing, she turned her head and found her nose buried in Jeremy's collar. The scent of Irish Spring cleared her head. Travelling against the mob wasn't helping their situation. Jeremy wavered.

"Steady there!" She squeezed to keep him upright as jolts of fear lit up her nervous-system.

"Not so tight–"

"Sorry." She let go of his stomach to hug his ribcage instead. He dropped several inches and walked with bent knees. With Jeremy being half-a-foot taller it didn't make hauling him around any easier.

Beth tripped over a passing foot. *Come on!*

"Hey! Watch out." The owner of the foot scowled. Jeremy counter-balanced to help keep them standing. More and more students and professors careened past, yelling and calling to each other; some carried stacks of books, others were on their cell phones waving their hands at people who couldn't see them, but all headed to the stadium just off campus. *Exactly where we should be going, too.*

"We're almost there," she assured. They were more than half-way across the asphalt path now. A faint ray of sunlight broke through the grey clouds and glinted off a modern-looking glass door above which the word PHARMACY was spelled in red block letters.

"There's an old guy with silver-streaked hair locking up." *That's not helpful.* "Wait!" Beth called. The bodies on the street absorbed her voice. It disappeared, much the same way she did in a crowd. "Mister–"

Jeremy winced. "–probably Pelbourne."

"Mr. Pelbourne! Wait!"

He turned. She waved wildly at him. The man dropped his keys when he saw them, a flash of disbelief crossing his face. Then he snatched his keys up and strode the last remaining steps between them. He looped Jeremy's free arm around his shoulder and helped Beth carry him to the storefront.

"Jeremy, what in God's name are you doing?" Pelbourne asked.

"My medication–" Jeremy leaned against the display window, trying to breathe slowly, deeply. His curls hung moist and limp as his long fingers left smears of cold sweat on the glass. Beth had never seen him this out-of-sorts, the cocky confidence gone. She pulled the jacket from him, back around her shoulder. The wind didn't cut into the shop corner as it had out in the open.

"My prescription. I need a refill."

"What am I supposed to do? They told us to leave immediately. There's an emergen–"

"*This* is an emergency," Beth said, following the pharmacist's gaze as he watched the mass of evacuating people; then he glanced at his watch.

"*Please*," she said. He had to help, for Jeremy's sake.

"Where are the pills I gave you a couple of weeks ago? The prescription's good for a month."

"Gone," Jeremy said.

"Gone?"

"Stolen from his dorm room," Beth clarified, assuming, but it sounded bad even to her ears. She hoped Jeremy's reputation ended with the ladies and didn't carry over into selling off his prescriptions. "It's been over…"

"A week." Jeremy provided, placing an awkward hand on Pelbourne's arm. His pale, icy eyes vainly sought a connection with the pharmacist. Beth squeezed her fists tight in the confines of her jacket pockets and stared at the man.

Mr. Pelbourne sighed. His keys jingled as he pulled them out again. *I should leave now. The pharmacist can help Jeremy.* And yet, Beth found herself resuming her role as a crutch while Pelbourne unlocked the store.

Inside, behind the drug counter, the pharmacist automatically reached for an empty bottle and the medication. Beth sat Jeremy down in a blood-pressure chair. She cringed at the grey wash of his face, making his eyes almost disappear.

"We talked about this," Pelbourne grumbled, glancing at the time again. "You can't forget about your medicine even if you don't need it as often any more. The diabetes is unforgiving – your body is struggling to access your insulin supplies. I–" He opened and closed his mouth a few times then shook his head. "I'm just repeating myself. I'll put a note on your file. We don't have time to do this properly. Grab a bottle of water for him, young lady, he's probably parched."

"Yes, Mr. Pelbourne–" they said together.

Back outside, Beth waved off the pharmacist's efforts to help her with Jeremy.

"Are you sure?" Pelbourne asked.

*No.* "We're gonna stop a minute so he can take his meds, then we'll catch up."

Jeremy finished a swig of water, "S'okay, Mr. P. We're right behind you."

The pharmacist glanced at his watch. "If I didn't have to meet my wife, I'd– She's a– Well, she worries and– You sure you're okay?"

Jeremy nodded. Pelbourne joined the wave of pedestrians heading for the safe zone. Beth turned, leading Jeremy to the parkette behind the plaza. Every nerve in her body screamed she was going the wrong way. They walked with the crowd to the end of the building then moved off toward the manicured green-space just behind.

"Careful, now," she said, lowering him to a wooden bench. She sat, too, and fought with the cap on his pills as he rested, head down, forearms on knees. Beth stared at him, so lost and alone. Where were his buddies? Did no one else think to check on him? A strange ache welled up in her chest. She swallowed, forcing it down before refocusing. Her freckled skin pulled with tension as the ribbed plastic bit into her flesh. The burn of it grinding against her palm made the image of the sexy red-head Jeremy followed from the restaurant pop to mind; the perky blonde he'd paced himself to meet outside the pub; and the dark-haired, dark-skinned, beauty leaving the dorm the day of her surprise visit. Each time her cheeks burned with embarrassment. *Why the hell am I here? Where are they?*

The cap popped. She dropped an Amaryl in his outstretched hand then swiped a tendril of light-brown hair from her face, locking it firmly behind an ear. Downing the pill, Jeremy then chugged the rest of the water. Beth tossed the empty bottle into a nearby bin.

Neither of them spoke.

She stared at his right ear.

He faced the ground.

The wind gusted past and he shuddered. Part of her wanted to slide over and wrap a protective arm around him, and the other part, well, she wasn't so sure he deserved her walking off right now. Perhaps a week ago, but not now.

"This isn't going to cure me," he said.

"Nothing will cure you. I'm not an idiot. It will help. You said it would help. Maybe I should take you to a medic if it's that bad."

"No. It doesn't work that fast. I've been off them a while now."

"It. Will. Help. Maybe I should get you another water." She stood, ready to search the shops nearby.

"No. I'm fine."

"You're not fine." She flopped down again, jamming her hands into her jacket pockets, wanting to stick her face in front of his to make her point but knowing the futility of it – of pitting her will against his.

"I will be. Besides, I need your help."

"As much as I should, I promise I won't leave you here. We'll go to the stadium toge–"

"I'm not going to the stadium."

"What?" *What now? I can't–*

"I didn't just go back to my dorm for the medicine."

"The medicine that *wasn't* there?"

"Right. The medicine that I knew wasn't there. I went back for my experiment."

Beth bristled. *You lied to me?* "Why? It's safe," she said, her voice clipped, edged with anger.

"Actually, it's not."

"What do you mean?"

He briefly massaged his temples with one hand. "My pills weren't the only things missing."

# ELEMENTAL FRICTION

NINE DAYS AGO

B eth walked through the student centre concourse with her book bag over her shoulder. Night permeated the skylights above, but no stars shone. It gave the shop-signs an over-friendly glow. The central clock read 5:45 p.m. in bright glowing numbers. She shook her head. *So few clocks actually have faces these days,* her mother's voice echoed in her head. Beth agreed, but the modern nature of the campus demanded large digital displays the profs could lord over their students when they arrived *late*.

Other patrons blurred by as Beth meandered past buzzing restaurants and pubs. Her stomach let out a hollow growl.

*I really don't have to go to my six o'clock tutorial. They'll only be rehashing the test. Besides, I'm sure I did fine.*

Hot cheese and pepperoni wafted from the Italian Eatery as spicy curry assaulted her senses from the Indian place next door. Music played over the intercom, *a Christmas carol maybe?* It was hard to tell and too soon to care. The indoor concourse warmed her face and hands so she unzipped her jacket. Beth's stomach growled, again.

The bright green, yellow, and white of the new Japanese Restaurant drew her toward its promise of spring and an all you can eat buffet. The blackboard sign claimed a meal for ten bucks, unheard of on campus. But the warm lighting and playful cherry blossom ambiance promised an evening without the threat of winter. Reeds and tall grass adorned the buffet tables, not overly crowded, as steam hovered between the food and heat lamps.

"Would you like to join us for dinner?" the host asked. His red hair and freckles vaguely familiar; maybe someone from her hundred-plus psych class?

Beth scanned the crowded tables along the right side of the restaurant. "Is there room?"

"I'll find you a spot. Come on." He grabbed a drink menu and a bundle of cutlery before skirting around the maze of tables and up the aisle by the buffet stations. There may not have been a lot of people getting food, but the place was packed.

The host chatted with a table of guys who gave agreeable grunts. *This is the only spot?* She glanced around. Nothing else available and no one she knew well enough to intrude on. One of the guys shifted his backpack to the floor and slid an open notebook closer to the pile of papers and plates littering the table.

"I hope you don't mind, Fridays are busy," the host apologized.

She shook her head to imply she didn't mind and sat. "I'll just take a water, please." He nodded and left. She smiled at the four students on the other side of the large round table. Her heart jumped a little, but she could do this. *Come on, first-hand insight into your final sociology thesis. Dive in.* She took a quick breath and channeled everything she could from her one theatre course last year into the moment.

"Hi, I'm Beth." She gave a half-wave. Her chest tightened, constricted her breathing. She held in what little air made it to her lungs.

"Jor-D." A big black guy with mini-dreads lifted his chin and winked.

"Moxie." His easy grin pulled Beth in. He ran a hand through his thick black hair, maintaining its wind-blown look.

"Wayne." He reached for a text book, flashing several tattoos at her. Nothing crazy, like skulls or flaming zombies, but nothing that stood out either.

The fourth guy with the dirty-blond hair, hiding behind his computer, didn't say anything. His attention so intent on his work, he'd zoned out.

"Hope you don't mind, we're TA-ing the same course. Need to hash out some stuff before Monday." Wayne pushed a few more papers around. Notebooks and texts of various thicknesses and states of use covered the majority of the table.

"By all means," she said. The un-named guy left-of-centre stayed focused on his laptop, typing, his curly hair, and forehead all that were visible. *Whatever. It wasn't the first time she'd been ignored and it wouldn't be the last.*

"Summertime" by Bon Jovi roared to life on the juke box as the words flitted across a large projection screen behind a small two-person stage. A microphone begged to be used.

*That's why it's so crowed. It's a karaoke restaurant.* Beth excused herself to prowl the buffet, her gaze lingering on the buff guy with the laptop and earbuds. *If you're at a karaoke restaurant, why listen to your iPod?* He probably wanted to stay tuned into whatever assignment they were working on. Wild karaoke could easily grate on one's nerves. She got the appeal of music and math but needed absolute silence for anything else. *Thank God I don't do math anymore.*

Returning with a full plate, Beth purposefully walked behind Laptop Boy's chair and stood close enough that he'd sense her presence. She was curious about his reaction and started building a profile of him in her mind. Staring down at the top of his head, the fullness of his shoulders made her think he was a gym rat. Catching herself being too obvious, she didn't linger any longer. Nothing. Not even a twitch, at least none she saw. Just a wash of algorithms and formulas on his screen. Beth moved to her chair, pulled it out with her foot, and sat down.

Moxie smacked Laptop Boy's shoulder with the back of his hand. LTB looked up and removed his earbuds. A woman's voice spoke from them but stopped abruptly. Beth frowned. *An audio book?*

"What formula did you use for that compound?"

LTB swung his laptop around, earbuds attached, for Moxie to see, and glanced up. "This one seems to work the best," he said.

Startled, Beth sat with a couple of long noodles dangling from her mouth. LTB's eyes appeared almost white. She slurped up the food before anyone noticed. *Light-blue – like a husky.* But she quelled the "superhero" quake the second she recognized it sizzling through her veins. Guys like him were off-limits, the same way movie stars and superheroes were. She could appreciate them from a distance, but knew well enough the impossibility of their reach. No silly childhood crushes for her.

"Hey, Jor-D!" Two more guys sauntered over, joining them at the table. "Ditch the drudgery, man, and grab some grub." Jor-D's plate had gleamed white since she'd sat down.

The new guys dropped their gear on two of the three remaining seats. Beth slid the last chair away from the table with her foot, pushing it against the wall before centring herself in the remaining space. She liked her elbow room, and six testosterone-filled guys was enough to breach even her capacity to hold out in the name of science. But she did. They forgot about her anyway. As expected.

For the next hour, the gang at the table ate and drank, becoming increasingly inebriated. She was no slouch when it came to packin' back a few, but not in public, and not without a friend to stumble back to her dorm with. And yet, the ensuing jocularity never reached LTB; at least, not until a curvy red-head sauntered past.

His head whipped up like a bull in heat. He actually closed his eyes and computer simultaneously, before standing to follow her. Beth caught a strong whiff of pear and cranberry. One of those Herbal Essences shampoos, or a cheap knock-off. It soured her stomach. She'd sat across the table from the guy for over an hour and he hadn't acknowledged her once.

LTB dropped some cash in front of Moxie, grabbed his gear, and ran his hand along the backs of the chairs. He timed nonchalant steps to align with Red's as she walked out of the restaurant. Beth watched the calculations in his steps with the way he held his body, adjusted his stride, and shifted his shoulders in a slight course-correction. This guy clearly had no qualms about chatting up the ladies. She filed that away, just in case.

LTB's cronies continued to whoop-it-up, each leaving to join a girl or two at another table in the span of about twenty minutes, taking their gear with them. The music changed from rock and indie to dance, with flat voices and even flatter personalities as they failed at stand-up between songs.

A large group walked into the restaurant singing American Pie at the top of their lungs. A quick scan revealed hers was the only table with empty seats.

She took the hint and left.

SEVEN DAYS AGO

Restless with the lack of progress on his bonus Chem assignment, Jeremy sat in the Graduate Lounge to clear his head. The patio was closed this time of year, but it still had the best draft on tap; besides he hadn't been in a for while and could use a pick-me-up.

Not half-way through the first drink, the click of heels on the bar floor drew his interest. A laugh tinkled out with a little squeak at the end, and the overwhelming aroma of vanilla and peaches floated with the girl as she walked past. Definitely her shampoo. Peachey's friend giggled a response as the girls sat at a small table just off the end of the bar.

"Hey, Wayne." Jeremy knew the bartender. They'd been taking the same courses for a few years, and both were specially selected this term to TA an overfull lab.

"She's a looker." Wayne's voice smiled.

"Make sure she's not thirsty."

"You got it, J. L." The glass Wayne held squeaked clean with a wipe before it clunked on the bar top. The tell-tale fizzle of a white-wine spritzer filled the air.

"Make it a peach twist," Jeremy said.

"On it."

The liquid gulped from the neck of the bottle seconds before a blast of citrus spiked the air as Wayne split a wedge of orange on the edge of the glass.

"The one on your right," Jeremy clarified, just in case Wayne was inept.

"Yeah, you know how to pick 'em. Sixth sense like a vampire." Wayne laughed as he walked over to the table, his steps echoing on the hardwood. Peachy giggled. The squeak was there. Jeremy didn't turn to acknowledge her, but he smiled. His cheek dimpled, the one facing her, and the skin next to his eyes crinkled slightly.

She took a breath from inside her glass and hummed. As Jeremy finished his draft, he listened to the click her tongue made against her teeth before she spoke about some gossip to her friend. He smiled to himself.

"You'll have to swing by later," he said as Wayne cleaned the bar top.

"Why's that?"

"Bet she's got that forever-stay lipstick on."

Wayne laughed, then leaned forward and dropped his voice, "Oh yeah. Don't want to advertise perfect red lip-marks on your face–"

"Ah, man, that's the price we have to pay. It's not so easy to scrub off waterproof make-up."

"It likes to hide behind ears and down necks where you'd least expect to find it."

"Ain't that the truth."

Peachy had two more drinks before her side-kick complained of a dead room. That's what he liked about Sunday afternoons, the Frosh were restless. Jeremy swallowed the last of his beer, popped a breath mint, and followed Peachy just a swing of the door behind as she and her friend walked out of the bar. The scent of her shampoo teased him around the corner of the patio.

*Four even strides and I'll brush her arm as I pass.* A sure-fire tactic for starting a conversation that would undoubtedly lead to an invitation to bar-hop. His trademark move.

The pierce of a cell phone fractured the air to his left – *traffic on the sidewalk.*

A sharp intake of breath – *female.*

"Oh, no," she said. The soft yet guttural voice shifted behind him and slightly to the left.

Flats with no traction slid on the pavement. Cell Girl

body-checked him from behind. Peaches paused a fraction of a step ahead. Jeremy stumbled into the patio fence, cussing. His arm burned. Heels clicked away as voices faded.

"Damnit." *It would have been a lot of fun to party with her. And who knows... ah hell.*

"I'm so sorry. With these books I can't walk, balance, and deal with the cell – are you all right?"

Jeremy stood up and shook it off, cringing at the sting along the back of his arm. "Yeah, fine. Don't worry about it."

"I feel awful. Look, they're just around the corner. You could still catch up."

He smiled ruefully, straightening his shirt, feeling for tears along his right forearm. His fingers slid over rippled skin. He rubbed them together. *No blood. Not too deep then.* "S'okay, maybe another time." He shifted and trailed his fingers along the edge of the wrought-iron fence.

"Ahh, okay." She sounded like she knew what he'd been up to. He tossed her a genuine smile, then turned and resigned himself to the dorm and homework. "Look, let me at least buy you a coffee–"

She kept pace with him as he walked. Actually, she bounced a bit on the balls of her feet. Every time she rose up onto her toes, he caught a familiar whiff of mint. *Her breath? Toothpaste?*

"I said, don't worry about it. No harm done." *I should take another look at that formula. The fuel compound–*

She stopped and lightly held his elbow, tugging at the tear in his sleeve. Her hand shook. "Are you sure? If I hadn't bumped you..."

He turned to face her and kept his eyes steady on the outline of her form. She shifted back. He'd breached her comfort zone. She stepped into the wind and he caught that same scent of mint coupled with... *clean soap*. The vague familiarity of it tugged at his memory, but he let it go.

"I insist, please," she said.

But that simple scent jogged his brain and got him thinking of the base elements he'd overlooked on his Chem project. *I gotta get this down.*

She followed, juggling her burden. The girl seemed nice enough, but wasn't his type. Actually, he wasn't sure why she was still trying to talk to him, and a small part of him felt bad for sloughing her off.

"I'm not fond of the coffee on campus. Besides, my dorm is just ahead." He tried to drop a hint, not wanting to offend or encourage.

She sighed. Not a deflated, lost-cause kind of sigh but not quite the pity sigh either. Something in between. It confused him. Why would she react like that?

"But if you want to come up to the common room, I could use some company." *Well, that came out wrong.*

"Company?" Had she heard it, too?

"I mean I– I have a project I need to–"

She laughed, somehow sensing the truth of his intent. "I've got some single serving Via's from Starbucks, if you've got the hot water," she offered.

"You have them with you?"

The tone of her voice intrigued him. She seemed like she could use a break but at the same time he detected something… *Is she playing me? Is there something more going on here than I realize?* Jeremy cocked his head in wonder. It wouldn't be the first time, but she didn't seem up to–

"Like you said, the coffee on campus sucks. I just order hot water and presto – good coffee."

Nearing his building, Jeremy paced himself and took a half-step left, swiping his access card over the reader. The door swung open with a faint hydraulic whoosh.

"After you," he said.

She slid over the threshold and stood by the elevator. He slid his finger down the wall then jammed the "up" button with his thumb.

"I didn't catch your name," she said, not exactly timid, more confused and apologetic.

"I didn't give it." The elevator doors opened. Jeremy entered and pressed the eighth floor. He could feel the closeness of the walls, made ever closer by her presence. Again, she shifted away. He didn't bother to look toward her. Her "bubble" of personal space was a lot bigger than the girls he knew.

"Well, you know mine. Though you've probably forgotten or whatever."

"I do?"

"Yeah, at the restaurant Friday… never mind. I'm Beth." He knew her hands were full, so there was no need to shake.

"Jeremy." The elevator dinged at his floor. The doors opened, and the common room before them exploded with chatter. The sheer number of people crowded in one place did nothing for him.

"Maybe we should hang in your room," she said, voice raised to be heard over the impromptu party.

"It's just down the hall on the end. Eight oh eight." He slipped along the wall, unlocked the door, and held it open for her; another first.

# ARCANE ELEMENTS

## SIX DAYS AGO

**B**eth glanced up from the chapter. She liked to walk around campus after a lecture, letting the sun and exercise warm her. *They keep those lecture halls far too cold this time of year.* A group from class walked a few paces behind her, planning to take the subway together for the fieldtrip to Union Station in the city. Their next project revolved around observing and predicting beyond established patterns.

Beth listened to their "established patterns" as they paid more attention to what they were going to do after the project instead of during. She could have easily slowed down by half a step and integrated herself into the conversation, but honestly, she didn't want to. Tired of trying to fit into pre-existing friend groups, Beth knew they'd only see her as a fifth-wheel. She didn't need "help" using public transit and she certainly wasn't interested in shoe shopping. Beth veered away on a less-travelled path just so she wouldn't have to listen to them anymore.

A group of guys laughing obnoxiously drew her attention. They stumbled toward Jeremy's dorm. Beth tucked the book in her shoulder bag, making a decision she was only half-conscious of. The guys flung open the door of the building so wide that it paused at its apex as if deciding whether or not to actually close... as if beckoning her.

*Maybe I'll surprise him. Let's see how he reacts to that.* Her final thesis was sound but only built on third-party stats. They'd left the door to Jeremy's suite open yesterday. The noise from the party in the common room had turned into an identifiable safety-net for her as they chatted over coffee. Sure, she'd been nervous, at first, but Jeremy exuded confidence even as he worked on his project. They talked about first year profs and the best study spots on campus. She'd never been that at ease around a stranger before and it confused her thesis findings. This would be a good time to do a little more practical research.

Beth jogged through the entrance before the door shut, and joined the idiots on the elevator, seconds before the door slid behind her. The number ten, top floor, lit up red. She pressed eight.

"–it's just like hot cheese!" the lanky guy finished his terrible joke.

"Ooo, that's what she said!" His friend punched him in the shoulder.

More laughter. Beth hugged closer to the exit, throwing up every barrier imaginable in the hopes they'd leave her alone. She hadn't appreciated the grabby hands of thirteen-year-old boys, and her view certainly hadn't changed with twenty-year-olds. Theses guys weren't like Jeremy. Sure, she knew he drank and had a "type", but he wasn't obnoxious or overbearing.

Smacking hi-fives ricocheted in the small space behind her. She closed her eyes and counted to ten. The doors dragged apart. Beth slipped between them, nearly launching herself down the hall. And there he stood, framed in his doorway. Godlike, his hip leaned to one side, palm resting in the upper corner. The image of five different "bad boy" movie stars (and one WWE wrestler) whipped through her mind before she had a chance to shake them out of her head.

The overpowering bitter-sweet scent of green apple pricked the inside of her nose. As her eyes watered, an oil-slick of a girl, scantily dressed, passed Beth and placed a small, stoppered, vial into her hand bag. The guys voiced an approving "heyyy" as she entered the vacated space before the elevator doors slid shut.

Jeremy looked through Beth.

She turned. *No one there.*

Beth gag-coughed on the residual traces of perfume.

He tilted his head, drawing his gaze toward her, but not quite focusing.

She gave a feeble wave, "Hi–"

"Beth?" He locked on to her, obviously still in a daze after his rendezvous. *You're such a moron, Donaldson.*

"I shouldn't have come. Sorry. I didn't realize–"

"Coffee?" he asked, disappearing inside his room. The door gaped open. Beth looked back at the empty common room, at the elevator, then his door.

"Why bother?" she whispered, but she let her feet carry her to his apartment all the same. She was doing this for science, for her thesis. *And it doesn't hurt that he's easy on the eyes.* She shook her head and pushed the thought away.

Standing in the very spot he'd vacated, Beth looked up at the lintel then down at her toes. Drawing her arms tight against the width of her body, she felt dwarfed even at five foot six. The room had an abnormally high ceiling and though the furniture was sparse, it overwhelmed the space. A large bureau met her chin immediately to the right. The tall double bed dominated the centre of the room, and a large window gaped without a shade above a built-in bench, showing nothing but a pale almond sky.

Jeremy sauntered through a door on the far side of the dresser to the en-suite, sloshing water inside an electric kettle. He bypassed his desk, nearly clipping his thigh. Next to the desk was another window and a long counter covering the remaining length of the wall, not two feet from the end of the bed; a surprisingly tidy bed all things considered.

"You can come in, you know." He plugged in the kettle, busying himself with what looked like a spice rack holding a variety of glass vials.

"Where to?" The chair overflowed with text books, mirroring the desk which also held his laptop.

"The bed's comfortable."

"You probably say that to all the ladies."

He laughed.

"At least the chair was available last time."

"Sorry. In the middle of an experiment. I need the space to spread out."

"So, the bed."

"Yup. I do need somewhere to sleep eventually."

Beth slid a step toward it. "I should have buzzed up. I didn't realize you'd– umm– have company over."

"You're company."

"You know what I mean."

He flashed her a wicked grin, tinkered with a glass vial, then turned around swirling it with his left hand.

"You gonna stand the whole time? Makes no never mind to me."

The kettle whistled softly. Beth leaned against the bed, the mattress groaning slightly. She rummaged in her bag for the Via sticks.

"Catch–" she said, holding up two small packets.

"I'd rather not." He pointed to the vial, now a deep blue. He walked over and she gave him the packets. Last time, she'd made the coffee while he'd washed out a scrape on his forearm. It had been awkward at first, but they'd launched into a one-up-man of embarrassing pet names and animal antics after she'd spotted his screen saver. It was a picture of his first dog standing nearly as tall as he was – a chubby little tyke with moon-shaped laughing eyes. His mom put the picture on the computer to personalize the gift. He'd never thought to remove it.

"I'm surprised you had class today. I usually plan my schedule to have Monday's and Friday's off. Four-day weekends are priceless."

"I don't have the luxury." She sat back a bit, letting the bed fully support her. "What are you working on?"

"My project for Chem Lab. That bonus assignment I was tinkering with yesterday. If it works, it's my key to grad school." Reaching into a cabinet under the counter he extracted two mugs with the York U crests half-worn off.

"Nice. Are you sure I'm not intruding?"

He chuckled. "What? Can't a guy multitask?"

"No. It's not in your genetic makeup. If you can accomplish coffee and swirling your experiment I'll have to officially register you as an anomaly – a freak of nature."

"Too late."

"What?"

"Too late."

"How's that?"

"Long story. Milk and sugar, right?"

"Yeah, but only a single." Beth slipped her shoes off and tucked her feet up. "You mentioned grad school. Are you graduating this year, too?"

"Trying to. I've taken a few extra years to make it this far. It's time."

Beth wondered if he'd switched majors or began by studying General Arts, but didn't want to pry. That's usually when things went south and she needed to follow this through for her thesis. So, she held her tongue, not letting herself linger over why she cared. Because she didn't. She was here in the name of science.

After setting the vial in the spice rack, Jeremy wiped his hands on his pants, picked up both steaming mugs and offered one to her. Accepting it, she breathed in the dark roast imagining game night back home in the winter and drinking a half hot chocolate and half dark roast coffee. It wasn't until she moved to the city that she realized it was a "thing" – *café mocha*.

She took a sip. "Mmmm… that's the stuff." He walked to the window with the bench on the far side of the room and faced out, his back to her again. "I never did ask before, but how did you manage to get a gig TA-ing a Chem class if you're still an undergrad?"

"I've got connections. And it helps that I'm the resident Chem genius. Wayne's my only real competition. He's a guy–"

"Yeah, I remember Wayne."

"Oh, don't get started on that again. We did not meet on Friday. We met yesterday."

"Wayne will back me up. Just ask him. It's not my fault you chose to ignore me." She laughed, enjoying calling him out on the snub.

"I was working!" Jeremy cleared his throat then continued, "But the Prof likes my ideas – she's the one I'm trying to impress with the bonus assignment. Door still open?"

"Yeah, I'll close it–"

"Don't bother. The floor's generally empty this time a day. So, Beth."

"What?"

"Beth, Beth, Beth."

"Jeremy, Jeremy, Jeremy."

"Is it short for Elizabeth? No. You'd be Liz I think if that were the case. Bethany?"

"Neither."

"What's left?"

"Don't laugh. It's a bit dated. My parents are weird."

His eyes kind of glazed over as if wishing his family were the good weird, then he took a sip of coffee and stared outside again.

"Spill," he said into his mug.

"Elspeth."

"Really?" He turned back to face the room but not her. No one ever really looked at her. "Well then, Beth just won't do. It's too plain. It doesn't match your personali–"

"Ha!" She snorted into her mug. "You so don't know me, and I certainly look the part. Beth's just fine, thanks."

"Why do you look the part? You're the only person I've met on this campus who doesn't fall into a category." He grinned into his mug before taking another sip. Leaning his back against the window frame, he looked up.

"A 'category'? You mean like Princess, Jock, Gossip, Doormat–"

He laughed. "Exactly."

"I don't believe you. I'd fit just nicely in the Quiet Nobody category. Besides, look at me." She pulled up a strand of medium length, straggly hair. "Light brown hair, light brown eyes, light brown freckles, and pasty pale skin. Now, that dark beauty you were entertaining before I got here, *she* makes a statement."

It was his turn to laugh. "Nothin' much upstairs, though. Belongs in the Princess category. Money, looks, and a free ride. Besides, I didn't say anything about how you look– Hmmm... *Elle*."

"What?"

"I'll call you Elle."

"Perfect," she muttered.

"You don't like?"

"Elle means 'she' in French. At least *Beth* gives me some identity."

"But then it should be Peth with a P. What's your middle name, then?"

"What's yours?"

He laughed again, sincerely this time. "Lawrence."

"J. L.?"

"That's what they call me."

"Who?"

"My prof's, the guys, my parents."

"Why did you tell me Jeremy, then?"

"You asked me my name, not my initials. What's your middle name?"

"Again, keep in mind my parents are insane." She rolled her eyes to the ceiling, he didn't register the inference. "Lenore."

"Ahh, Le-*nore*. Should I call you 'shadow girl'?"

"N-o-r-e not n-o-i-r. Although, if it was in me to be the black sheep I would, but you're wrong again. I'm just too normal and totally sibling-less."

"Elspeth Lenore... E. L.... El. Sorry, there's just no getting around it. Elle it is. There's a mysterious quality about it that works." He downed the last of his coffee and set his mug on the counter before walking around the bed and standing in front of her. "And I don't believe you."

"Don't believe me what?"

His legs brushed her knees. There was no space between them to breathe. Her heart jumped. *What's he doing? Why's he standing so close?* Her eyes dropped to his hands, placing her mug on the dresser behind him... making their way toward her. Bobby and Johnny Denton's hands flashed through her mind. Truth or dare. The closet in Marjorie's basement at her thirteenth birthday party. Those grabby hands.

"Plain. You say you're plain." He reached out and caressed her shoulder, lightly gliding his fingertips along the length of her neck to the base of her ear, and along her jaw. *What the hell?* She gave an involuntary shudder... but this time, not in disgust. *Oh shit. What is this?*

"No!" Beth shoved him. He stepped back, bumping her mug with his elbow. She ran out, sock footed, slamming the door behind her.

# REVELATION

FOUR DAYS AGO

Beth sat on a wooden bench by the university's main fountain, dry now since the days had shortened. She ate leftover fried rice from the previous night's dinner, intending to mull over the paragraph from her all-important Soc thesis she'd been working on. It dealt with perception and first impressions. She sided with the postulation that first impressions were lasting ones; what the senses beheld in the first few moments of an initial meeting, the brain then retained. It analyzed all further information according to a pre-devised internal stereotyping inherent in everyone.

Beth had gleaned a lot of first impressions over the years, and knew all too well how pitiful her own firsts were. She tried to change that during Frosh week and year one, but either she came across too clingy or too aloof. University sucked. Either you attended with a bunch of people you already knew, or fell into a clique during frosh week. She'd chosen to work instead of party. Really, Beth was her own worst enemy.

Her thoughts drifted back to the Japanese Restaurant that first night, and then the incident with Jeremy outside the Lounge. She squeezed her eyelids tight until they hurt, then she looked out at the field. *His actions are constantly contradictory, but my first impression was correct all along. He's only interested in himself. A man-slut. Nothing deeper. Don't know why I thought there would be. I should be thanking him for proving my thesis right.*

Usually, in the spring and early summer, Beth would lie on the bench reading and listening to nature. It was a mild Wednesday for early November; all but the wind had deserted her – even the grass seemed greyer. Her winter boots lay abandoned beneath the bench as a mild breeze dried the sweat from her socks. Two sets of footsteps approached from behind.

"It's her," a guy said.

"You said that last time."

"I can see her face this time. I'm outta here, man. You deal with it."

Stabbing a mushroom, Beth thought about her term paper. It wasn't due until next week, but it was integral to graduating with summa come laude. She had this figured out now. She'd been right all along. Yet, some distant part of her wished he'd proven her wrong.

"Elspeth?"

Jamming her fork down, she slid to the far end of the bench. Beth made sure he could hear her unspoken "*what?*" He stepped closer.

"Get lost, Jeremy." She jammed her feet into her boots.

"Elle, wait." He dropped a heavy plastic bag on the bench.

She stood up.

"Elle–"

Grabbed her stuff…

"Elle, I'm blind."

… and left.

TWO DAYS AGO

*It's just another line. An excuse. A way to get me to drop my guard again. I've turned into a project to him, just like that damn experiment he's always working on.* And yet, she still mulled it over two days later, after her last tutorial.

A hollow rumble echoed in her gut. She did not feel sorry for him, she was hungry. Fridays were the one night of the week she allowed herself campus food. The memory of a ten-dollar meal drew her, books and all, to the student centre concourse.

Moving through the covered walkway she got jostled by the on-coming traffic, and then the guy behind her stepped on her boot, pulling it off her heel. She stutter-stepped trying to wedge it back on as she detoured into the main building. Weaving in between tight groups standing around talking just to get out of the cold, she forced her way through the crowd. Her nerves ratcheted up every minute as shoppers and talkers bumped her and broke into her personal space. She shouldn't have been surprised.

Normally, it didn't bother her this much, but today everything did.

"Would you like to join us for dinner?" Freckle-boy greeted her again.

"Hi, Tom." He frowned a little and cocked his head sideways. "Beth, from Psych. We sit in the same row." She held out her hand. He shook it, but his expression remained blank. Nothing new. "I overheard your name when you passed me in class to get to your seat this morning." His eyes widened slightly and he smiled vaguely.

"It's busy, but a couple just left. Come on." He picked up a drink menu and cutlery package. "This way." She followed him past the buffet services to the back of the room. They meandered in and around several tables until he motioned her to one directly opposite the jukebox. It sat in the far-right corner about four tables away from the stage. *A small table for two. Perfect. No interlopers.* She put her book bag on the chair in the corner as three girls leaned toward the microphone and finished their song.

"So, hit me with your best shot! Fire awaaaaaaaaaaaaaa-A-hay!" Polite applause broke from the immediate tables surrounding the stage. Beth draped her coat over the chair opposite her books, then slid her wallet into the back pocket of her jeans. Straightening her teal campus sweater, her favourite, she eyed the empty stage. Everyone stuffed face or hauled ass back to the buffet tables.

The smell of tempura shrimp wafted to her from the closest table. Her stomach clenched and gurgled. Food would have to wait, though. The stage was lonely –

microphone half-in half-out of its holder, blank video screen, and a stray napkin someone had left near their table. After pigging-out on the buffet, there'd be no way Beth could sing. She'd probably puke.

Snaking through the tables, she found the song list on a podium by the jukebox.

"Country, Reggae, Hip Hop, Soft Rock... Hmmm... No, not tonight." She flipped to the last page and found Pop. "Ahh, yes, Christina darling." She punched the number sequence into the jukebox and took the stage.

Christina Aguilera's image from her greatest hits album flashed on the screen with the song title. A techno-coloured swirl danced to the rhythm as the first words appeared. But she didn't need them. Beth rolled up her sleeves, shook out her ponytail, and took a wide stance behind the mic. She grabbed the upper stand and tilted it toward her.

"After all you put me through, you'd think I'd despise you – but in the end, I wanna thank you. 'Cause you made me that much stronger–" She kicked her foot out at the beat change. A gritty, guttural voice, akin to Christina's, woke up the microphone. She saw nothing but the back wall, actually, she didn't even really see that. Her eyes glazed and in her mind the music video played.

Beth belted out line after line of Christina Aguilera's "Fighter" as her heart walloped her ribcage. For four minutes and nine seconds, her voice echoed throughout the restaurant, down the concourse, and into the rafters, vibrating the skylights.

But when the music and applause melted away, so did any recollection of her. As Beth wound her way through the tables to the buffet, the usual snatches of conversation reached her.

"Do you know her?"

"Hey, where'd she go? That was awesome."

"No, the girl with the *black* hair. By the stage. *She* sang Fighter."

What could she expect though? People were hungry, they were stuffing their faces; this was a restaurant not a concert, and that was both her opener and closer.

Beth heaped her plate with shrimp, pork kabobs, rice, and a bunch of stuff she couldn't recognize.

An Asian guy sang Achy Breaky Heart, getting egged-on by his friends, as she slid back to her table and onto her chair. While she unravelled her fork, ignoring the chopsticks, a shadow fell across her from behind.

"If that hadn't been so well rehearsed, I'd have thought you were sending me a message."

Beth stiffened. Ignoring him, she stabbed a deep-fried breaded piece of shrimp and chomped down onto it. Jeremy stepped around her and found the chair opposite. She watched him tilt it forward, take notice of the weight, then feel for her book bag before setting it under the table between them.

He sat.

She stared at him, tempted to lean forward and wave her hand in front of his not-quite focused eyes.

He didn't respond to her stare or the uncomfortable tension between them. But he did drop a heavy plastic bag on the table, narrowly missing her plate.

"Hey!"

"I thought you might want your shoes back."

Beth looked at the bag. "Those are mine?" Leaning over, she snatched it up, and put the bag on her lap.

"Can I explain?"

"You already have. I prefer to eat alone."

"Now, that I don't believe. You may not want to eat with me, but you don't want to be alone." His comment pierced her heart.

"Go away, Jeremy." She stuffed more food into her mouth, more than necessary. Not that he could tell. Besides, what could he possibly know about what she wanted?

"I thought you knew – thought that was why you were trying to 'be my friend'. I thought, thought it was a pity-play to make you feel better about yourself or whatever. There's always a reason."

She stared at his eyes and squinted a little as she chewed. He looked at her. Right at her, but not quite.

"If you're blind, how did you find me in the park the other day? Tonight?"

"Coerced Wayne to look for you. Said he'd recognize you."

"Yeah, not surprised."

"I know. I remember what you said about seeing me here. So, I waited for you. Heard the song. Caught your scent–"

"You stalking me now?"

"I could have said the same about you earlier this week. Elle–" He leaned forward.

"I have a scent?"

"Everyone does." He leaned back but left his hands flat on the table. "Can we talk?"

"I'm busy."

"You're eating. Hear me out." She picked up a meat kabob without looking. "First off, I apologize for invading your space. I forgot how personal a reading can be. I use my fingers to–"

"I know." She swallowed. "I mean, I've read some stuff and TV, movies. You don't have a cane," she accused.

"I do, but I don't need it. Not around here anyway. I've mentally mapped out the campus. Most of it anyway. Been here for six years, going on seven. As long as I stay to my mental paths I'm good." He sighed, his entire posture changed suddenly and he looked away again, like he always did.

"I had a bad experience during frosh week and ended up abandoned in a field surrounded by nothing but forest. Anyway, I don't tend to travel at peak times. My profs expect me to be late and leave early." He straightened up then leaned forward, resting his forearms on the table. "At the fountain, when Wayne and I were looking for you, instead of tracking my steps I keep a sense of where I am by walking shoulder to shoulder with him. I can feel the density of space change when I walk by a tree or person. Here, too. And see vague shadows–"

"All those times– I thought you were just arrogant, didn't look at me because... you know, no one ever does."

"I try not to look right at people. I try to hide it. I just never expected it to, well, to work... even though I always hope it does."

"Great. I'm the only moron who thought a blind man could see. I feel so much better." Beth dropped her fork on a now-empty plate and relished in watching him jump at the noise. She wanted him on edge, the way he made her feel.

"Well, I appreciate it."

"How's that?" She took a sip from her water bottle.

"People look at me and see the disability. You didn't."

"I don't think you'd appreciate what I do see."

"You were still nice... everyone else has an ulterior motive."

"I probably did, too." *I know I did.* Beth pushed her plate away, gulped more water, and grabbed her stuff. "What does it matter, Jeremy? Just pretend we never met. I'm not your type anyway. This was a mistake."

She never should have tried to test her theory. Never should have bothered with him or anyone for that matter. It never worked out anyway.

Beth manoeuvred to the front of the restaurant to pay. Jeremy came up beside her just as a cute, blonde waitress, smelling like strawberries, swiped Beth's debit card. Elspeth watched him from the corner of her eye. His nose twitched but he didn't follow through.

"I can't pretend," he said.

She punched in her code and collected the receipt. "I'm leaving, now," she said and jogged out of the building.

Beth stopped half-way back to her residence in one of the glass-shrouded walkways and opened the plastic bag.

*Yep. Those are my shoes.* But stuffed into each opening was a bouquet of Starbucks Via instant-coffee sticks. A strange ache needled her heart but she swallowed a few deep breaths and forced it away. She had no idea how long she'd stood there, staring at the coffee in her sneakers.

Time just didn't make sense. Or maybe it wasn't time but something else.

Someone walked up behind her.

"The next morning, when I found your shoes, I knew I had to find you." Beth turned to face Jeremy. He ran a hand through the hair at his temples. "I haven't had a friend in a long time. It was nice. The company."

"I wondered… I was curious. I don't know, maybe I did pity you because I didn't want to pity myself. I don't know what I thought I saw last Friday. I sat down expecting pretty much what I got. The guys putting up with me, ignoring me after being suitably polite. But you… it felt different. It didn't feel like a snub but it had all the classic ear-markers. You're a contradiction, Jeremy, and I'm a sociology major. You really can't see anything?"

He shook his head. "Not since I was ten, clearly that is. Undiagnosed diabetes… a rare case of type two. There were complications. It's that long story I mentioned before, when you called me an anomaly. You weren't wrong."

He was looking at her, yet his eyes remained unchanged. There was no clarity of recognition, no twinkle of amusement. After tucking her shoes into the book bag over her shoulder, she stared at him again, at his eyes – but closer now, less than two feet away. The closeness didn't seem to bother him, even though it electrified her blood. She didn't usually get that close to people. Pale blue flecks feathered the light-gray of his irises. Scanning his face, she saw no trace of a smile, a twitch, or other tell. *He really can't see anything?*

Beth turned and kept walking. He joined her, their

shoulders a hands-breadth away in a surprisingly comfortable silence. The light of the lampposts flickered and faded as they walked from beneath one to the next, skirting around the interior walkways between the buildings. A light breeze brushed her hair away from her cheeks, cooling them. She counted her steps. No reason. Well, maybe just to see what it was like. She turned to face him when they stopped outside her residence.

"I suppose it's only fair," she said.

"What is?"

"I can see you. If you want, you can read my face."

"You sure? We can be friends without–"

"I overreacted." She snorted. "I more than overreacted given the situation. My experience with 'worldly' guys is limited and… I really didn't know you were blind." He didn't laugh at her or her definition. She didn't want to call him a player to his face, that'd be rude. But she'd seen the flicker of recognition, and something else.

Beth lightly held his hands. Jeremy's long fingers could have mastered the piano. She fluttered her own digits as if they were the keys before bringing his hands to her face. Jeremy took a half step closer. Her electrified-warning kicked in along with something else. It was strange being this close to a guy she barely knew.

She studied his features again: brows furrowed in concentration, one eyebrow slightly raised as his fingertips followed the line of her jaw. Tracing her ears, he placed loose strands of hair behind them, sending a shiver through her at the delicate nature of his touch.

Defining the shape of her face, he explored her hairline then followed her cheekbones to the bridge of her freckled nose. She closed her eyes. A tingling of tiny pressure points traced the frame of her lids, slid down to her nose, and peppered across her lips, lingering a moment – charging the air between them.

When she opened her eyes, he was less than a breath away.

# ANOTHER KIND OF MEDICINE

ONE DAY AGO

**B**eth lay on her bed with both feet in the air surrounded by printouts, every coloured highlighter in existence, her laptop, and her favourite pen, but she couldn't concentrate. Even after twenty-four hours, the feel of Jeremy's light, probing touch sizzled across her cheeks, around her ears, and down the sides of her neck.

He'd been so close... did he have any idea what that did to her? Maybe he expected it or not at all because he obviously wasn't interested in her that way. *Oh, shut up, brain!*

She rolled over onto her back, grabbed a teal highlighter, and shaded the new sentences that outlined the entire thesis for this paper – for her life: *First impressions are lasting. The brain internalizes the emotional and physical responses creating neural pathways that will then continue to be accessed whenever identifying with that particular person. Once the pathways are "set", it's incredibly difficult to alter those initial perceptions, and most people won't try to.*

Beth scratched it out, sighed, then circled it again before burying her head in her arms. What the hell happened with Jeremy, then? She was certain her first impression had been negative, and yet after the follow through…

"I don't get it."

"Don't get what?"

Beth jolted upright sending half of her papers and several highlighters scattering to the floor.

"Jeremy? What– What are you doing here?" She cranked her head to look around the corner of the open doorway and watched Cathy, her roomie, sashay down the hall to the common room.

He stepped into the small space and pulled a white cane out from behind the wall where he'd been leaning, slowly walking in. Flopping down across from her on Cathy's bed, he retracted the cane into a longish-pen and shoved it in his back pocket.

"Are you busy?" A wrinkle creased his brow and he didn't even give Beth a second to respond. "I can't believe that guy. The nerve!"

"What guy?" Beth gathered up her loose pages and shut them inside her laptop, still reeling at Jeremy actually being there. In *her room.*

"Wayne. We're standing with the other guys chatting with Professor Young who casually asks about the re-working of the formula on the first-year lab, and he pipes up with, 'We hashed out that one as a team and came up with a viable alternative to explain during tutorial.' I mean, can you believe that guy? The nerve."

"Yeah, the nerve."

Jeremy cocked his head at Beth and squinted in the awkward silence. Beth knew he saw through her.

"Okay. I give. I don't get it. That sounded harmless enough," she said.

"Harmless? Hardly. 'We' didn't come up with Jackshit. I worked it out, shared my idea with Moxie and then Wayne gives the info to Jor-D after–"

"You mean at the Japanese Karaoke Restaurant two Fridays ago?"

Jeremy suddenly looked like he'd sucked on a lemon.

"I was there, remember? Oh. That's right. You don't." She tried to tease but her jittery nerves made it sound more like an accusation.

"Right. So, it was *my* computation. 'We' had nothing to do about it and now Wayne looks like the star pupil because he's the one who spoke up, making it look like his idea even though it was all mine. If I go to the prof and set things straight, I risk looking like a sore loser instead of team player, while Wayne gets to play the hero for working out a simpler way to teach the newbies. I'm screwed no matter what."

"Wow. That sucks." Beth shifted her legs around underneath of her for the third time, unable to get comfortable.

"What's wrong?" Jeremy asked.

"What? Wrong? Nothing."

"Bullshit. You sound different. And normally we've started working on coffee by now. What is this, a double-standard or something?"

"The kettle's in the–" She glanced at the Ikea drawer on wheels that sat under the window between the two beds and realized Cathy hadn't returned it to the common room after all. Then, what Jeremy said finally clicked in her brain. "Wait. What? Double-standard?" She stood up, checked on the water level, then plugged the kettle in.

"Yeah. You've been uptight since I got here. What? Do you have a guy stashed under your bed I don't know about? 'Cause I'd know about it." He pointed to his ears and gave her one of his cocky smiles.

"No! Hey, I think you're channeling your alter ego. That's got nothing to do with me."

"Then what's the deal? Why the cold shoulder?"

"I'm not giving you the cold shoulder." She pulled two mugs from the top drawer and set them beside the kettle before turning and smashing her fists on her hips in indignation.

"Again, I'm calling bullshit. I can hear it in your voice."

"You're in my room," she blurted, then gave a shaky laugh at his confused expression.

"So, I was right. There is a double-standard. You can pop by my place unannounced but it's not okay for me to show up unannounced at yours."

Beth went from shocked, to confrontational, to thoughtful, and embarrassed in less than a second. Jeremy must have sensed it because he laughed.

"Admit it. It's a societal double-standard. Women want

to be treated as equals and it's no big deal if a girl drops in to hang with a guy, but when the opposite happens–"

"We barely know each other," she said, and realized she'd still gone to visit him after knowing him for less time *and* had thought nothing of it. Just that she had to prove her thesis. What if he'd actually been a schmuck and had taken advantage of her? That's what she'd assumed, right? But if she really believed that, she'd never have… and yet she'd still assumed he was coming on to her. Beth grabbed her head and folded herself in half with a groan.

"Exactly. And yet you still–"

"I know. I know. But it's a stigma society will never get past."

"Really? The sociology major is telling me that we're doomed to repeat our mistakes? Then how can anyone fight for equality knowing that stigma will always be there?"

"This is different. Men and women–" Beth stopped herself, not even sure what she was going to say and poured the via sticks into the empty mugs. She clicked off the kettle before the bubbling turned to whining.

"It should be. If you're expected to behave yourself in my room, then the same courtesy should be extended to me when visiting your space. There shouldn't be anything awkward about it."

"Considering your history, I could easily take your intentions the wrong way. Any girl could see this as you making an advance."

"Like you did when I tried reading your face the first time?"

Beth blushed. He hadn't been trying to make a pass at

her. But was he really just joking or was this one of his tactics for lowering her guard? *You're not his type!* She poured the water, added their condiments – *condom*ents. *Shit, even normal words have my brain spewing the stupidest things.*

"Here." She handed him a mug then sat down beside him, her jitters suddenly gone with her brain's assessment of this very innocent happenstance.

The guy needed to vent to someone. He couldn't go to Moxy or Jor-D because they'd tell Wayne and probably get upset that Jeremy wasn't willing to play nice and share the credit with the whole team.

"Are you sure Wayne is being an ass about this?"

He blinked at her change-back in the topic then said, "Definitely. There was a twinkle in his eye."

Beth punched his shoulder after he took a sip of coffee.

"Whoa, hey! This stuff's hot."

"A twinkle in his eye? Really? Now who's full of shit?" She turned to face him, folding one leg under and letting the other dangle over the side of the bed. He shifted to face her better and gave her a mischievous smile.

"I *heard* it."

"You did not. Wayne is your bud. God, he even took off an afternoon just to wander around campus with you looking for some girl, just to give her shoes back. Now who's reading too much into things? Come on, let the team have this one and don't take it so personal."

Jeremy glanced at her over his mug just before he took a sip, and smiled. She knew his husky-dog eyes couldn't see her, only shadows, but it still felt as if he did.

"Now, about that double-standard," he said, and they launched into an hour-long debate on the equality of the sexes and the societal expectations that stood in the way of true advancement.

# PERCEPTION

TODAY

Beth sat up on her bed, growled, and threw the crumpled version of her latest thesis across the room. Cathy ducked her blue and purple shooting-star locks out of the way then stuck out her tongue.

"Hey! I'm not a target, you know."

"I don't know what to do!"

"About the hot guy? Tap it, girl."

"No. Keep it in your pants, will you?" Beth pushed past the blush heating her ears. "My thesis. I basically had to rework the entire thing. Now, it feels like a bunch of crap. But it's true. But I don't have any stats to back it up. Shit. My paper is due at the end of the week. I have to go digging through periodicals for the exact opposite data I searched for the first time around." Beth flopped back onto her pillow and crossed her arms over her face. "This is impossible."

"Just go with your original thesis. You proved it, right? Its what your prof expects, right?"

"But I know it's wrong," Beth's voice came out muffled. She let her arms flop down crucifix-style. "I'm dead."

"You don't have to be."

Beth lifted her head and repaid the comment by sticking out her own tongue. Cathy smiled sweetly then raised her Kindle e-reader in front of her face, showing off her middle finger. She didn't mean anything by it, but it never earned her any bonus points either. Beth's roomie didn't believe in paper textbooks, everything was digital. Rolling over, Beth crinkled the notes beneath her. She liked to consider herself a hybrid, bridging the gap between print and digital, but even that was hypocritical and obsolete thinking. How could she say *save the trees* in one breath, and ask for notebooks and pencils in the next?

Nothing made sense to her anymore. Two weeks ago, she knew exactly who she was and where she stood. Now... her thoughts drifted back to shaggy blond curls, a chiselled jaw, and a devilish grin that made her skin tingle. *Stop confusing the matter.* Beth had forced herself into Jeremy's life to prove a point. *How shitty is that?* He saw her as a friend. *Friend.* Cathy's voice echoed, *hot guy.* What was she going to do about him? He stopped by to talk, yesterday. Nobody did that anymore.

*You did.*

"Arugh!" Beth grabbed her hair and pulled hard. "I need air." She stood up and grabbed her jacket from the closet at the foot of her bed.

"Sure you do," Cathy taunted from behind her reader.

"Shut up."

Beth had to figure this out once and for all otherwise her graduating average was screwed.

She never saw the stairs down to the main floor, her body worked on autopilot until a blast of cold air brought her back to reality. Hazy, indistinct clouds glazed over the morning sun. She glanced at her watch. No one would be up this early on a Sunday, not that 10:00 a.m. was early. At least she could get some research in relatively undisturbed, emailing herself notes.

But, instead of heading to the library and pouring over periodicals to see if anyone else had stats on first impressions that matched hers, she found herself walking in circles along the paved outdoor paths. She watched the occasional person or group hurry from one building to the next. A few study clubs and religious services were going on, but nothing else. Well, maybe hangover concoction cures. Lone figures huddled into faux-fur-lined hoods with ear-bud wires trailing down to hand-filled pockets.

She recognized the odd face here or there but didn't bother to nod or even wave – they weren't looking her way. Gia walked by with her arm looped through Mike's, their faces huddled close as their breath frosted in the air. Beth knew Gia from Musical Theatre last year. She was nice, but then she was nice to everyone. Beth had even considered ignoring her resolve not to bother making friends this late in the game, but had purposefully missed the signs. Sure, Gia talked to everyone and made you feel important and special in that moment, but her invites to hang were always parties you'd get lost in; her questions about how you were doing never dug deeper. She was nice, but she already had her core group of friends. She didn't need any more.

Beth's had chosen to ignore her instincts with Gia, her first impression. She couldn't afford to do that with Jeremy, too. The thought made her stop walking mid-step. Someone bumped Beth from behind.

"Oh, my God. I'm so sorry," Rene said, catching her shoulder bag as it slid from her arm to the ground. "I gotta go. Call ya back, soon," she said into her cell phone and then pocketed it. The T.A. assigned to grade Beth's section of the alphabet in Sociology readjusted her burden and then squinted at her. "Elspeth? You okay?"

"Yeah, fine. I'm sorry. I didn't know you were behind me. Lost in thought."

"Not out for a brain refresher, are you? The Soc paper driving you mad? Only a week left."

"I know. I don't know. I mean, I'm second guessing things."

"This late in the game? I gave you the only ninety percent on the thesis outline. You have a solid angle. What's up?"

Beth looked past Rene and took in where she was for the first time. She'd done eight or more circuits around Jeremy's building. So much for going to the library. She closed her eyes briefly and shook her head before making eye contact with Rene again.

"Hey, don't worry about it. You've got this nailed. Trust your instincts." Rene's phone flourished like Tinker Bell's wand. She glanced at the caller ID. "I gotta take this. See you in class tomorrow."

As Rene walked over to the Bethune building, Beth knew what she had to do.

He was playing her.

That's what guys like him did. Everything she thought he'd proven wrong was just another illusion... another angle for a different challenge – her. She'd set herself up for this and when he took the bait, so had she. He didn't have any feelings for her, he was playing the long game.

*Time to prove my thesis right.*

Beth did an abrupt-face and headed straight for Jeremy's dorm.

No more games.

# AN HOUR INSIDE A MINUTE

## LATE MORNING

An abrupt knock made Jeremy tense a little before Elle said, by way of a greeting, "I finally figured out why you want to keep me around." He smiled at her second unexpected arrival that week, then focused on moving his experiment away from the sink just as the kettle whistled. "The coffee's addicting and I'm the only dealer on campus," she said.

"That's a coincidence. I'm making Mr. Noodle." He stepped away to give her room, the foot of his bed pressing into the back of his legs. Something was off about her voice, but he couldn't place it.

"For breakfast?"

"It's almost lunch."

"Well, not anymore."

He sat on the edge of the bed, smelling a vial in his hand. He was so close to figuring this out. If she'd popped by ten minutes later, she would have missed him. As soon as he got this nailed down, he'd be at Professor Young's office with his notes. He scrunched his nose, not sure what he smelled anymore.

"Save my soup some water. I haven't eaten in a while."

"What's *a while*? Is that why you're so pale? I'll fix you right up." She bustled around his kitchenette, clinking mugs and prying open the dried noodle bowl.

"Lend me your nose?" he asked.

"Excuse me? I'm afraid it's attached." Her easy banter tugged another smile from him. She was fine. Whatever he thought he'd heard was gone. Jeremy cocked his head to the side then rose and walked over to the large window opposite his door. A piece of tinfoil rested on top of the bench by a hammer, right where he'd left it. Using an eyedropper, he placed a daub of his now glutinous experiment on the foil. After capping the vial, he picked up the hammer.

"Come here."

"What are you doing?" She shuffled over but didn't get too close. Somewhere in the back of his mind he wondered what she might do if he did get closer. Instead, he whacked the foil. Once. Twice. It sparked, popping the air like a cap-gun. She jumped. "Jeremy!"

"What do you smell?"

"What the hell–"

"What. Do. You. Smell?"

She sniffed and moved beside him after all. The warmth of her body radiated their nearness – far closer than she usually stood. He lingered in the moment, then shook off the feeling. He didn't do feelings. Girls were just a fun distraction. Beth took advantage of his hesitation to steal the hammer away and set it on the counter behind her.

"I don't smell anything. Why?"

That was a good sign. He reached around her to grab an identical vial from the spice rack by the sink.

"And this one?" Jeremy popped the top, dropped a dab on the foil then tried to juggle the tubes while reaching around her for the hammer. His body pressed against hers stirring something more inside him. Elle wasn't like the others, but he caught the hitch in her breath at their closeness.

"Jeremy! Ask for help."

She brushed past his beltline to try and reclaim the hammer just as he swung it. It parted the air in front of his nose then hit the foil. *Crack!*

She jumped against him, knocking them onto the bed. He breathed in minty soap, torn between wanting her and wanting her answer.

"And?" he asked, holding her loosely in his arms, trying to keep everything from spilling.

She sniffed toward the small reaction by the window sill, still lying next to him. His skin tingled, fingers itched to drop both vials and run them through her hair. But her body didn't curve into his. Her hands, hovering so near, didn't go searching like many others had. And yet, he suddenly found himself wanting her to.

"Bad eggs. Why?" Elle slipped off the edge of the bed and set the hammer on the extra wide window sill.

"Sulphur. Good." He followed her, shifting his weight from one foot to the other, but lost his balance getting up too fast. "Head rush."

"Jeremy, sit down. Don't drop that stuff. What were you thinking?" Beth guided him back to the side of the bed and moved to stir the coffee, the metal spoon clinking rhythmically. "Here." Heat radiated from the mug she tried to hand him. He shrugged and held the two vials up. Beth took the smelly one, the failed attempt, and replaced it with the mug. He wasn't letting his successful experiment out of his hands.

"Your soup is still steeping. Crunchy noodles suck. Start with that." She turned away. The crackle of the lid flipping up then back told him she checked on his lunch again. *Is she avoiding me?*

"Smelling this stuff all morning, my olfactory nerves went numb. I needed a fresh nose. I fixed it, Elle. I won't get into details, but the liquid needs to be cooled then allowed to react with the catalyst and a sharp, blunt force to ignite. Standard combustible engine stuff. I spread the catalyst on the foil just before you got here." As he sipped the coffee, he continued to stir the air with the promising vial – his breakthrough. "I just need to add this information to my notes. I'm so close to this Masters approval I can–"

The hall intercom squawked, "Please remain calm. This is an emergency evacuation. Make your way to the stadium immediately. Please remain calm. This is an emerg–"

"What? An evac?" Beth sighed and shuffled across to the door. "Let's go. Come on, Jeremy." The siren from a bullhorn splintered his ears. The message repeated again. Elle took his coffee. Two mugs thumped the counter. Liquid splashed. She leaned over, pulled him up and dragged him around the bed as he moved to set his experiment down...

⚓

A band of filtered sunlight wavered ahead in the mostly-dark passageway as Beth raced with Jeremy away from his dorm building – the evacuation alarm now a faint, intermittent wail.

Beth inhaled deeply. "I see daylight." The old tunnel set up for students to get to and from the dorms to the main buildings gave her the creeps. The ancient graffiti echoed its forbidden nature. Apparently, Jeremy's mom had worked out access to the passages on his behalf. He'd sounded both miffed and appreciative about that.

"I told you we were almost out," Jeremy said, leaning against the cool, moist concrete. Beth turned to face him, hugging herself and pulling her jacket tighter. The threat of an emergency made her stomach roil, as had the closeness of Jeremy's body when they'd landed on his bed. But worse, because she liked it.

"Come on, we're almost there."

Jeremy's voice fell flat. "If you say so. The stadium's still half a block away."

Beth backed up toward the faint light wanting to get out there. "You can rest later. I don't want to get harassed by the cops. We need to find out what's going on."

"No one will harass you. We've caught up to the crowd. I can hear them."

She shuffled another step away. "Come on, Jeremy."

He rested his head against the concrete, then rolled his

skull back and forth before leaning forward with his hands on his knees. He sighed. "I have to go back."

"What? You can't. They'll have cops crawling all around campus by now."

"I– I need my meds." *That came out of left-field.* He stood, but wavered before catching himself against the wall. She had no idea what to expect when she walked into his dorm this morning, but it certainly wasn't this.

"Get them later, when the threat's over." Every nerve in her body screamed at her to get her ass back in gear and get out of there.

"Can't." Pushing off again, he stumbled back the way they came.

"You'll get caught. You won't see them coming. It's not worth it."

"I have to try."

"Why? Why now?" she half-yelled, frustrated by his stubbornness.

"I forgot to take them again. I got distracted. It happens when I work sometimes. I was going to take them when I got up. I don't need them all the time, and I thought I was doing okay. But now– I need to go back."

"Then I'll come with you." She gritted her teeth and shifted to follow him. He really didn't look well and would need–

"No."

"No?" She stopped. Beth didn't like his tone. She'd never heard him like this before.

He sighed, but didn't turn around. "I can't ask you to put yourself in danger. Like you said, we don't know why they're evacuating. I'll meet you at the stadium."

"Where?"

Walking forward a few steps as if to bridge the invisible barrier between them, he paused and said, "Back entrance. Stay on the left side and I'll find you. I gotta go."

She watched as his form grew indistinct and then blended into the shadows. The sound of his footsteps echoed back long after she lost sight of him. *What in the world has gotten into him? If he needed his meds so bad, he should have grabbed them before we left.*

Beth kicked a rock and sent it skidding down the long access tunnel. She swung around and stepped toward the light. Nearing the opening she stopped short. Muffled voices and the sound of hurried strides filtered through the shrubbery outside. She looked back over her shoulder, slowly her torso and hips followed her head. Beth moved away from any sightlines near the mouth of the passageway and paced to keep the chill from settling again, rubbing her arms over her jacket sleeves. *God! He's so infuriating.*

"One week," she said. "Nine days in all actuality, but this?" She shook her head. He was an anomaly, to be sure, but did that mean she should go? "You don't just abandon someone in the middle of an evac, Beth," she said and looked out again, then back down the dim tunnel. She jammed her hands into her jacket pockets. The alarm screeched beyond the shaft's opening. She winced.

*Just go. He told you to go.*

*No.*

Her gut said stay, even though she knew Jeremy was perfectly capable of getting to the stadium on his own.

She growled and whipped her arms around the confines of her coat, fighting to contain her frustration.

Beth glanced at her watch – *fifteen minutes.* Sighing, she kicked another stone then turned to face the opening of the tunnel as she paced. A few tendrils of creeping vine wavered back and forth as the passage breathed in its slumber. A plaque denoting the year of its construction clung just inside the entrance, lit by hazy sunlight. But she didn't read it.

Jeremy said this was one of a network of tunnels buried beneath the campus – passageways for students to get from building to building in bad weather, but no one used them anymore. Now, the spaces between the original structures above were occupied by modern expansion and glass walkways. One building melded into another making the ancient system obsolete... and dangerous. There was a reason they'd been sealed up. Stopping, she stared at her shoes and wiggled her toes under the worn leather of the tan-coloured sneakers. Her favourite pair.

Four days earlier she would have sworn she'd lost them for good. She would have sworn she'd never be standing in an abandoned tunnel waiting for a guy whose only use for women was to have a good time. She'd come back this morning looking for answers but all she'd found were more questions.

Beth leaned her head and hands on the cold concrete wall. "God, Jeremy. What the hell's keeping you?"

# VERTIGO

## HALF AN HOUR AGO

Moving at a sluggish jog, Jeremy retraced his steps back to the dorm. He stumbled over his own feet and cussed, staggering slightly. He managed to find the wall to steady himself and the nausea subsided. Speed walking was marginally better, but his brain seemed to swim in a vat of tequila. And he wasn't drunk. He punched his thigh.

"Idiot."

He'd been meaning to refill his prescription when he couldn't track down his meds last week, but the Chem project took priority and it slipped his mind. He'd gone five days before and had been all right, but this time he hadn't been eating properly.

"Moron."

One day turned into two, which turned into a week. It was easy to forget when distracted. Even Elle could see a difference. His mind refused to focus and he found himself lingering in the memory of that morning. He slogged back along the tunnel as he remembered the feel of her laying in his arms.

Jeremy pushed his fists against closed eyes.

"Ahhugg! Damn it." That's not what he needed right now. He forced his brain to track her movements after the first evacuation notice. She'd pulled him to the door, but he couldn't remember what happened next. Food deprived and lacking insulin, he'd had to rely on Elle as they left. They'd taken the stairs across from the elevator and then he'd shown her the tunnel access door. But what about before that? What about when they'd been standing there in that split-second between grabbing their coats and rushing out the door? He had to remember or he'd actually have to find a way back into his dorm room to check. *It has to be in the spice rack.* There'd been no time to lock it up with his supplies under the sink. There'd been no time to hide anything.

He'd tried to go in the bathroom – she'd pushed him... grabbed his arm? *No, that was in the hall for the stairs. It could be on the dresser or even the bed.*

"Ouww-Ch-a." He dropped to all fours, knee throbbing from banging it against the wall. Jeremy wiped his hands on his pants. Using the tunnel for support, he stood up again. *Come on! Focus on what you're doing, man.* His stomach flopped and his head swam. He stagger-stepped.

The density in the air changed and the drip from a ventilation pipe echoed as it landed in a puddle. Pacing his strides, he walked to the opposite side. A handle grazed his knuckles. Opening the basement door, the air from inside sucked back, resisting. He listened carefully, resting his forehead against the cool metal.

No more warnings.

No talking.

No creaking.

*No— There.*

The pop of grout between ill-fitting tiles. Someone was on the next level up. Jeremy carefully shut the door then staggered to the gated staircase another thirty-two paces along. It led near the side of the next dorm.

He squeezed out from between the bars at the top of the tunnel, crouched and waited by the hidden open-air entrance. His bomber-style jacket scraped against the concrete. Listening carefully, he mentally mapped out his surroundings: pigeons cooed to his left, elevated slightly; a hill with sparse trees; footsteps paced to the right but mostly behind the tunnel entrance; one pair, echoing slightly from the building ahead of him. A muffled incessant thuwp of chopper blades attacked the air some distance above and behind the target building. Seven paces. It would take seven paces at full stride to reach the side of Wayne's dorm and four more to swing around the back to the fire escape.

The footsteps returned. Jeremy timed the interval as they swung around and paced away. He did this three times. *Two minutes.* If he ran, he'd likely draw attention to himself and smack into the side of the building. That wouldn't be wise. Rising, his knee buckled, still sore from getting smacked into the concrete of the tunnel. He fell against the upper support of the stairwell. After righting himself, he shook his head to clear his mind. The footsteps made their turn.

*One. Two. Go!*

Careful when placing his feet on the asphalt, he sustained an even cadence. Jeremy raised his hand about two feet from the building and then traced it on the brick around to the back corner. The cool iron-flaked paint chipped into the air as he ran his hand over the lower railing of the fire escape.

*One-hundred and forty-five seconds left.*

Climbing, he channelled any cat-like abilities he might possess, including powers of the sixth sense, if they existed. His heart timed the countdown of the patrolling feet's return while his fingers tracked on one hand the number of steps he mounted, and on the other hand the number of floors passed.

*One and a half stories at zero.*

He stopped. Inhaling deep calming breaths, he urged his heart to slow and hush. The breeze blew brisk up here, chilling his face. Stuffing his hands into his pockets, he listened. The steps reached their apex. *Was that a longer than normal pause?* His lungs screamed for air. His legs trembled. The footsteps softly walked away. Releasing a controlled breath, he continued to take even inhalations as he climbed another eight and a half stories to the roof.

Luckily, he'd been up here once before. Granted, once wasn't nearly enough to be cocky about, but enough to remember. Jor-D, Moxie, and Wayne convinced him to party up there for Jor-D's birthday last summer – when Jeremy's lack of sight was still a novelty to them. The guys had let him pace out the perimeter, where he smacked into a metal stair rail opposite the fire escape. They'd said it was a truss connecting the two buildings, for emergency evacuations only. While Jeremy had chosen to sit by the door to the internal stairwell most of the party, he never forgot about that truss.

At the top of the ladder, he belly-crawled over the rim of the roof and dropped down. He couldn't remember the exact pacing to the opposite side, but was certain it couldn't be more than twenty. He fumbled for his collapsible cane but it wasn't in his back pocket. Elle ushered him out of his room so fast he didn't have time to grab it. After those estimated twenty strides, Jeremy raised each foot and used it like a cane, testing the way ahead.

The night he and the guys were up here, they'd brought deck chairs, music, girls, and coolers full of drinks. Campus security found them about two hours after the party started and shut them down. Jeremy got to leave with the girls. Since he was blind, security had exempted him from clean-up. He'd gone back to his dorm with a cranberry-beauty that night. But for some reason, the memory of that conquest didn't rouse him like it used to.

His toe tapped the metal rail. Moxie said the truss looked like a three-sided triangular ladder suspended from one building to the other, flat side up. So, it was reinforced, but the ground still extended a long way down. Jeremy grasped the chill rails and hauled on them, just in case. They didn't budge. Leaning over the rim of the roof, he explored the patterns and contours of the ladder with his hands. A gust of wind swept up, pushing against him.

Not good. He had no idea what to expect once he crossed over, but he had to do this.

Wiping fresh sweat onto his jeans from his palms, Jeremy pushed up the sleeves on his jacket and grabbed the rails. Placing his foot on the first rung, he forced a breath of air out of his mouth before breathing in again through his nose. Jeremy gritted his teeth as he hauled his body up onto the truss. He wavered, sensing almost nothing beneath him. Crouching lower, he tried to compensate. Each rung was approximately a foot apart. Jeremy began to count – one, two, three... sliding his hands, and lifting his knees and feet in succession, methodically.

Jeremy focused on the words and the pain of his shins. He didn't think of the one hundred feet vibrating below him, the air very much alive as it whipped around. Curling his long fingers Jeremy gripped, released. His shoulders ached with suspended tension. The arch of his right foot cramped. Inhaling sharply, he lay flat on the truss, elevating his foot until the pain subsided. *Seventeen. How many more?* His mind raced.

After having broken his leg when he was nearly eleven, tripped on a curb of all things, he'd been forced to admit his sight was failing. Not only did they confine him to a cast, but he was diagnosed with Type-II diabetes. Not Juvenile Type-I, but a rare case of youth Type-II. Apparently, he was too fat. He'd been two-hundred pounds at the time. Walking with crutches needled his underarms, making his arms constantly numb. If he'd wanted to move, which he hadn't, a metal walker was the only thing he could use.

Even while he was healing, the doctors wanted him "active" and not confined to a wheelchair. The grips on the walker bruised his hands, bit into his flesh. He never wanted to experience that again. While he was no longer overweight, his grip had strengthened. The force with which he held the rails of the truss echoed the pain of that fat little boy.

Squeezing his eyes shut and grunting softly, he hauled his body up and continued his count. Eighteen, nineteen, twenty… His knuckles scraped the brick of the other roof at twenty-five. He froze. *Now what?* Shit. He didn't trust himself to turn around and land on his feet, even this close to the roof. Jeremy's arm wobbled and his fingers ached webs of dull pain spidering along the back of his hands and up his forearms.

He let out two pent-up breaths then inhaled and held the air in his lungs as he walked his hands over the brick ledge and down the side toward the roof. His heartbeat deafened him as hot spikes of pain shot up his forearms from the death grip he had on every surface. After caterpilling his body over the edge, hugging tight to the wall, he lay on the pebbled roof curled in a ball. Steady, regular breaths helped calm his nerves as he worked the kinks from his hands.

After walking his body up the side of the roof wall, he stood as far from the waist-high ledge as possible without losing contact. The two buildings were identical so he used the same pacing from Wayne's to locate the access door in the middle of the roof.

Resting his forehead against the rusted door, Jeremy calmed his breathing. If there was a patrol unit still sweeping his building, the last thing he wanted was to alert them by panting down the stairwell. Stepping back, he tugged the handle.

It didn't budge.

*What? No!*

Jeremy grabbed the cold metal with both hands and hauled back with everything he had. The door groaned before releasing. He stumbled but held on. The echo of the moan called down the stairs as he stepped in. *Dammit.* Sliding his hand along the rail, he followed it down two floors. Jeremy slipped inside the corridor, closed the door, and listened. Nothing but the drip of water from the leaky tap in the common kitchen on his left. He turned right and hurried to his room.

The door remained wide open, as instructed. Jeremy slipped inside and ran his fingers over the top of his dresser. No vial. The sleeve of his jacket snagged on a drawer pull, scraping it open and jostling the bureau. *Shit.* Jeremy unhooked his sleeve, shrugged out of the coat, and tossed in on the bed.

He checked the window by the fire escape. Nothing. He checked his desk. Books; portions of braille titles speaking to his fingers, but still no vial. He bumped their half-full coffee mugs with the back of his hand and sent them clanking into the small sink. *God dammit! Jeremy. Get it together.*

The rack on the back of the counter held two, three, four samples, but the fifth was gone. Just as he reached the opposite side of his bed and the window seat, the metal stairwell door crashed open. His heart lodged in his throat as he dropped to the floor. The sightlines from the stairs, across from the elevators, went straight through his room and out this window.

"I'll take left," a gruff, official sounding voice said.

"Right."

He grabbed the foil, crumpled it into a ball, and shoved it in his pocket as he flattened himself to the floor. Jeremy listened as the cops cleared the common room and then each took a connecting hall. He couldn't steady his breathing. Blood pulsed past his eardrums as he strained to hear how long it took for the officer closest him to sweep a room. It was too quiet.

*Shit. Shit. Shit.*

He slid the hammer into the bench drawer under the seat, with the rest of his tools. The last thing he needed was for the cops to find the remnants of his project. Or him. But he couldn't figure it out. He had to chance it.

On all fours, he crawled on the floor, sweeping his hands under the bed and around the counter. Jeremy knew his meds weren't here. That's not why he came back. The missing test vial a few days ago, the suddenness of this threat – whatever it was – and Elle's reaction to the practical test... so many "friends" dropping by this week out of the blue. It all equalled bad news.

Then he heard it. Boots scuffing the thin hall carpeting going into the room beside his.

*I can't get caught. This is my fault and I have to fix it before my life is ruined.* Jeremy felt for the window ledge, released the lock, and cranked the full-length window open. It creaked.

*No!*

Heavy footfalls.

He dove out the eighth-floor window, landing hard on the metal mesh platform of the fire escape. Reaching up with one hand, he shoved the window closed and hugged his body against the building below the frame. The breeze snatched all sound, distorting or hiding he wasn't sure.

Jeremy had no idea how long he lay there, shivering in just his blue polo sweater, waiting to be found... but no one opened the window.

No one yelled at him from below.

No one knew he was there.

# COUNTER MEASURES

## TWENTY MINUTES AGO

The metal from the lower rail of the fire escape bit into Jeremy's palms as he dangled above ground he couldn't see. First year he'd studied the schematics of his building, using the text-to-speech software on his laptop, before systematically mapping it out in person. He'd jumped from below the landing of the fire escape a few half-hearted times, never actually touching the lower rung, hadn't really expected to. He was no Michael Jordan. Tall, maybe, but not an athlete. The fact the retractable ladder on Wayne's building's fire escape was permanently down was not a coincidence, but no one had tampered with this one.

*Come on, J. L., do the math. Six feet tall plus a minimum two-foot reach past your head, only another two or three-foot drop. It's nothing.* But the steel digging into the joints of his fingers was real – the distance to the ground only theory.

*Get your ass in gear! The cops are already suspicious. Now jump!*

He let go. His stomach tried to force its way up his esophagus. The ground came fast, jarring his whole body, but he didn't fall. Taking a step toward the side of the dorm, arms outstretched, his legs gave way. He stumbled into the wall, scraping his hands in the process.

*Stupid diabetes.*

Bracing his back against the wall, Jeremy fought past the hollow feeling sucking his marrow out, struggling to maintain control. He listened for the patrol's steps but nothing came.

*Oh, crap.* The cop could be anywhere, and the longer he stayed put the more likely someone would find him. And he couldn't afford to be found. Again, he waited, listening.

Nothing. Not even the wind.

At least if he'd heard something he could plan and coordinate for counter measures. Now, he was just blind. And that pissed him off. The guy on the ground might have been called to investigate the commotion Jeremy caused on the eighth floor, might have been planted at the door looking out, or the lot of them might have moved on to the next dorm – which he highly doubted since there were still two floors to sweep plus the roof.

*I can't stay here. If they're still in the building, they'll probably check the perimeter one last time before moving on. I gotta risk it. I gotta run.*

Jeremy peeled his body from the side of the building and stretched his neck with a head roll. Listening to the environment one last time, he squared his shoulders in the general direction of the tunnel, and ran.

As he sprinted over the asphalt and brick walkways every sense remained on high-alert. No one yelled. No one chased after him.

CRACK.

Jeremy stumbled back, rubbing the left side of his face. Another newly planted oak where there hadn't been one before. *Damn campus restoration project.* He staggered around the young tree, hands up to keep from hitting anything else. Stumbling forward, he searched for the shrubs hiding the south side of the tunnel opening or the rough concrete of the entrance. *I can't be that far off.* A laser of panic sizzled through him, igniting every nerve. *Where am I?*

Footsteps and voices breached the open air behind him. *They're done searching the dorm.* Jeremy tripped over his own feet as he pushed himself forward, arms sweeping ahead. Then he felt the bushes and instinctively turned right, crouching low until he slunk around the tunnel opening and into its moist, sheltered interior. He leaned back against the wall and tried to catch his breath. Jeremy rubbed his face with one hand and pushed himself away from the wall with the other. *Gotta keep moving.* But the jolt of adrenaline leached from his body. He collapsed to all fours.

*Shit. I need my meds. I can't fix this without them.*

*You can't fix this alone.*

But Jeremy knew Elle was already gone. Waiting for him at the stadium, where he wasn't going anymore. Not now that he knew. Everything added up to a shit-ton of trouble. Someone knew about his not-so-theoretical project. Someone who knew his habits and used this evac to slip into his room and take what wasn't theirs...

His insides squished Jell-O-like, and the ache in his gut intensified. The voice of his high school kickboxing coach echoed through his brain, "Get your fat ass up and do it again!"

"Get your fat ass up," he grunted, leaning heavily against the wall and stumbling to his feet. *Get to the pharmacy. Get your meds, and figure this out.*

Sliding his fingertips along the cool concrete, he passed the basement access to his building. Forcing one foot in front of the other, he retraced the path he and Elle had originally taken when evacuating. He hadn't wanted to leave through the main doors. Too crazy. And Elle had grabbed his arm so fast, he didn't have time to get his gear. Now, he was cane-less and jacketless.

*Elle.* He sighed. Some dark place inside keened, knowing she was gone and would stay gone when she found out this was all his fault. Jeremy hadn't simply talked with anyone in years, not since his buddy Josh graduated "on time". With Jeremy taking fewer classes each year, based on which texts he could order in braille, he couldn't graduate in four years with the rest of his class. Seven years. And now, if they linked him to this scare, never. His chance at a mentorship with Dr. Young obliterated.

His toe hit a stray rock, knocking it across the formed concrete beneath his feet. The echo of the skitter carried throughout the tunnel.

"Jeremy?" Elle whispered softly. His heart leapt.

"Elle? You stayed?" He collapsed against the wall and held his head. *She stayed.*

Elle touched his arm. "What's wrong?"

"Lack of insulin– catching up to me. Making me nauseated. Weak." He dragged in a mildew-laced breath.

"We have to get to the stadium. I'm sure they'll have medics there–"

His chest constricted the breath as he choked out, "No." He couldn't afford drawing attention to himself, getting stuck at the stadium, being *found.*

"What?"

He wanted desperately to explain, but he couldn't do that to her. Couldn't risk putting her in that kind of danger. He owed her that much at least.

"No. Just get me to the pharmacy. I need my medicine."

"It wasn't in your room?"

Jeremy heard the accusatory thread in her voice as he pushed himself from the wall. *Get your fat ass up!* He stumbled forward a few steps. His knees gave out. *Shit!*

"Okay! Just give me a minute."

Jeremy wanted to say no again, but he couldn't. He couldn't do it on his own. Squeezing his eyes shut, his heart and brain battled over how much to tell her, what to say or not. *God J. L., why didn't you listen? Keep it theoretical, not practical.*

Elle unzipped her coat and knelt down beside him. Loose gravel scattered at their feet. "Put your arm across my back and grip my left shoulder."

He placed it over the coat.

"*Under* my coat, Jeremy. The temperature has

dropped. Wind chill."

He carefully slid his arm across her back. Her body radiated warmth. He followed her smooth contours beneath the thin cotton sweater. A similar heat roiled in his groin. He hadn't been this close to her since he'd read her face the night she finally let him apologize, and falling on the bed together this morning didn't count. That was an accident.

The jacket pulled tight and tugged against the strain of two wearers. She shifted closer to his lean torso, not a fat kid anymore, and turned her head toward him as she draped the open half of her jacket across his back. The tip of her nose brushed cold against his ear. He startled at the nearness of her, suddenly unable to separate the pull of his hormones from the ache of his body's need for insulin. Just being next to her infused him with renewed strength.

"Grab the sleeve. Slide it on if you can. Make sure your shoulder's covered." Elle slid her hand across his back. Fresh mint and clean soap lingered on her skin and hair. He couldn't risk pulling her into this insanity. He had to do this alone.

Her fingers searched for the best grip to help him up, even as their bodies crushed against each other.

He'd fix this alone, once he got his meds and his body equalized again. *But you know it's not instantaneous. You know this won't fix everything.*

"Ready? Now."

Jeremy struggled against the weakness in his knees and towered over her. He hunched his shoulders to try and minimize the distance between them. She led him to the opening and the ivy, crisper than its summer counterpart, it scraped his cheeks and forehead as they left the tunnel to a blast of cold air and a rush of voices.

"Wait. I can't see yet," she said. Jeremy stopped as the hazed world before his eyes brightened but never cleared. He glanced over at her. A dark shadowed-splotch blending into the pale haze.

"Where's your pharmacy?" Elle asked. He faced forward again.

"Other side of the bushes."

"Have you come this way before?"

"Yes." Jeremy smiled, but without heart.

"We're surrounded by nine-foot hedges. Which way?" She turned their bodies looking left and then right.

"Through. It thins a bit to the right." He vaguely waved his hand, knowing she'd see it soon enough. They all did.

Elle walked with Jeremy over a slight rise in the grass. On the slope down she said, "How on earth did you find this spot?"

"I've had a lot of time on campus to discover the best routes to and from certain places. *This* was a happy accident in my second year."

"Something tells me this isn't the first time you've stumbled over here with a girl."

He grinned at her. A tease. She knew he entertained a certain "type" whose high-heels made for poor all-terrain shoes. But those girls just kept him from getting bored… or at least they used to. A blast of cold air gripped his spine, making his body quake. As they pushed through the evergreen shrubs, the musk of cedar and pine clung to their clothes and lingered in their hair.

Jeremy stumbled over the curb, having lost count of his steps. Elle's strides were slightly longer than his as he struggled to compensate for his usual number of steps from the hedge to the shop. She tightened her grip around his waist. He dug his fingers into her shoulder as he staggered, dragging them into the noise of the crowd.

The onslaught of voices and the crush of dozens of bodies made Jeremy stiffen. Too many people. Too many mixed signals. They jolted forward and staggered again. He hated feeling useless. Hated having to rely on anyone but himself. But Elle knew he wasn't just some charity-case.

"There's an old guy with silver-streaked hair locking up. Wait!" Elle called. The people on the street absorbed her voice. "Mister–"

"–probably Pelbourne," Jeremy winced.

"Mr. Pelbourne! Wait!"

The pharmacist almost didn't believe them, but something made him unlock the shop where he started yet another lecture about Jeremy's lack of attention to his health. Getting distracted by a paper or prepping for the class he TA'd or even a test might consume Jeremy's attention for a few days at a time – slightly skew his insulin absorption when he forgot to take his meds. But this was different.

Elle tried to explain but something in her voice sounded like she questioned herself for trusting him. Jeremy couldn't afford to have Pelbourne follow her train of thought. Luckily, he didn't. Pelbourne put a note on Jeremy's file, handed him the prescription, and walked them out of his shop. Thank God, he didn't press them about going to the stadium together. It would be hard enough convincing Elle to leave him. She hadn't the first time… had waited for him in the old tunnel. But not this time.

Elle turned, leading Jeremy to the parkette behind the plaza. The cold air bit at his exposed flesh, now that she'd reclaimed her jacket and they were back outside. His knee buckled but she caught him.

"Careful, now," she said, lowering him to a wooden bench. She sat beside him, not too close, and struggled with the cap on his pills as he rested his head in his hands.

The click, click, click of the childproof bottle echoed in his brain, a clock ticking a countdown for which he didn't know the time. And time was running out. This was no scare, it was the real deal. But even as Jeremy thought of all the places he had to check, he recoiled at the monolithic task – challenging enough for any normal person… impossible for a blind man.

The cap popped. Beth dropped an Amaryl in his outstretched hand. The space between them practically thickened. She watched him as he downed the pill and chugged the rest of the water Pelbourne insisted she grab before they'd left the pharmacy. Beth stood and threw out the empty bottle.

She came back and they sat in silence. Her knee brushed against his. He sensed her eyes on him again.

He hung his head.

A gust of wind passed and he shuddered. Even healthy, there was no way he could get around campus undetected. He needed his strength back. He needed to see.

"This isn't going to cure me," he said, more for himself than anything else.

"Nothing will cure you. I'm not an idiot. It will help. You said it would help. Maybe I should take you to a medic if it's that bad."

"No. It just doesn't work that fast. I've been off them a while now. Haven't been eating right..." He should have been paying closer attention. *Who had taken them? How many uninvited guests had stopped by this week?*

"It. Will. Help. Maybe I should get you another water." She stood.

"No. I'm fine."

*I can't do it. I can't ask her.*

*You have to! There's no other way.*

"You're *not* fine." She flopped down again, jamming her hands into her jacket pockets, the air between them charged, electrified.

"I will be. Besides, I need your help."

"As much as I should, I promise I won't leave you here. We'll go to the stadium toge–"

"I'm not going to the stadium."

"What?"

"I didn't go back to my dorm for the medicine."

"The medicine that wasn't there?"

"Right. The medicine that I knew wasn't there. I went back for my experiment."

"Why? It's safe." Her voice came out clipped, edged with anger.

"Actually, it's not."

"What do you mean?"

He massaged his temples with one hand, then stopped. "My pills weren't the only things missing."

# FORMULA FOR DISASTER

NOW

"You mean the experiment that blows up?"

"Shhh– yeah. That one. I– I need you to help me. Be my eyes on this one–" Jeremy's insides twisted, and not from the meds. *She's the only one I can–*

"How do you know it's gone? You can't…"

"See?"

"Exactly."

"Has that ever been a problem for me before?" His ire grew. He knew his room inside and out. Elle was supposed to be different… "It's not there."

She went quiet. He felt the air thicken between them, pushing them farther apart.

He sighed. "Look. You know what a small amount is capable of. That was a pin-drop. The whole vial is gone, as well as the catalyst. The only people who knew what I was doing were you and the guys."

"What guys?" Her voice dissolved into the space before

her. He tried to picture her looking out, toward the stadium. Tried to remember what freckles looked like. His dad's arms had been covered in them, more so in the summers.

Jeremy ran his fingers through the hair at his forehead then let his hand drop to his lap.

"My TA Partners, Jor-D–"

"Moxie and Wayne."

"Yeah." She'd only met them the once, but never failed to remind him she'd been there that night at the all-you-can-eat restaurant, when he hadn't noticed her. Maybe he had. He thought about that night far more than he should, always wondering about that lingering presence behind him at the table. Still, at least she knew the suspects.

"Why would any one of your friends want to have you thrown in jail?" Her voice changed trajectory, toward him. "It doesn't make sense."

"I only met Jor-D and Moxie last spring when we were interviewed for the TA positions. They're post-grads."

"So, it must be one of them?"

"No, I don't think so."

"Wayne! No way. He helped you find me, works with you on any number of projects. You're always talking about–"

"We're both competing for an apprenticeship with the same prof for our Masters. Wayne doesn't 'work with me' on anything. He gets frustrated and then asks me for the answer. He slides me a freebie at the Lounge Bar whenever he's on shift because he's trying to stay on my good side."

Jeremy had never allowed himself to think like this, let

alone say it out loud. He'd tried to convince himself that Wayne wanted to be "buds" – but it was true; Wayne used Jeremy just as much as Jeremy used him. Now, that silent truce was gone.

"Do you honestly believe that? I saw him with you– Smiling, laughing, helping… stuff friends do."

"Maybe."

"We don't even know why the campus is being evacuated. You can't just assume the worst. What if this has absolutely nothing to do with you? With your experiment?"

"So, what am I supposed to do? Just turn myself in on a fifty-fifty chance that I misplaced a highly explosive, illegal, chemistry project and hope I don't lose my one chance at graduating into a Masters Program? Or at all? I've been here for *seven years*, Elle. I'm not ready to just throw all that away."

Tension electrified the air between them. She hadn't moved in some time. He knew, without a doubt, that she was staring at him. He stared right back, hoping his gaze connected, hoping it was enough to make his point.

"Okay," she finally said, more determined than he'd expected. "Then let's find out for sure."

❧

Beth joined the waning crowd meandering to the stadium. Most of the people on campus today were likely already safe inside. The early afternoon light remained just as hazy as it was this morning. *God, that was a life-time ago.* The scattered groups of students were in no rush. Clearly, they didn't think this was an actual emergency. She tried to remember the name of the girl Jeremy claimed could get her back out again: *Shantaya? Shenice? No… Shaunika.*

She walked beside a cluster of friends, heads and cellphones together – talking and texting updates.

"680 News is just repeating that we're in lockdown. Not even the police sound-bites give any detail." Beth watched as the girl flipped her screen and selected another app.

"My mom said there's only an automated message linked to all the phone lines," a young guy added.

"The website just keeps flashing the same warning over and over again," another girl said.

"What about your brother? Isn't he dating the guy in the Student Centre–"

"Yeah. Nothing. The cops aren't saying squat to anyone but the upper echelon."

Still, no one knew what was going on. Beth slowed her steps and let the group get ahead as they rounded the sweeping curve to the stadium's main entrance. Three cop cars, lights flashing, and two black vans flanked the double-wide metal doors leading in. Beth slowed again. Someone stepped on the back of her shoe.

"Watch out," the guy said and tried to deke around her, bumping her shoulder in the process. But she wasn't paying attention to him, or the others. Several cops kept going in and out of the back of one of the vans, checking in with the group of officers standing between them. Beth stepped onto the grass.

"No joy from the south quadrant."

"What did Simmonds say?"

"Hasn't checked in yet."

"Excuse me, Miss, but you'll need to step back onto the path."

Startled, Beth looked up into the imposing face of a female officer. "Oh, I'm sorry. Yes. Of course." And she fumbled her way back into the crowd. *So much for overhearing anything from the source.* Through the doors, one officer stood to either side watching the flow of students. They reminded Beth of the Buckingham Palace guards who were never supposed to smile or break formation. She'd get nothing outta them, either.

Beth moved with the others through the chill of the building, up the ramp, past the vacant food booths, and out into the second-level stands. The density of voices crashed into her ears. She raised her hands to block the sound as she looked around, still walking with the flow of incoming students as they circled the bleachers.

The stands were full of multi-coloured jackets and hairstyles. Just as many groups chose to stand as sit. The football field seemed to have a gravitational pull for staff and administration. She caught sight of a familiar face, and risked looking over her shoulder a little too long.

"Whoa, there. Watch where you're going," a male officer said, gripping her shoulders, and steering Beth away from one of the many exits on this level.

"Oh! I'm so sorry." She stepped out of his reach, then turned back. "I don't suppose there's been an announcement about what's going on? Why we needed to evacuate?"

"No. No announcement yet."

"Will there be one?"

He smiled but it didn't reach his eyes. She was clearly not the first person to ask.

Beth raised her hand and shook her head, motioning for him to just ignore her. *Well, so much for Plan A.* She scanned the masses of students surrounding her and realized for Plan B to work, she'd actually need to find someone who gave enough of a shit about her to talk to her. At first, when she arrived at the university, she tried to find a crowd to run with, but they all had history somehow. So-and-so knew that person from high school, those guys met at an upgrade course over the summer, they were dorm-mates and competed as a team during Frosh week... And even if Beth got a smile and an invite to join a group project, nothing ever went beyond the logistics of class. *Shit, Jeremy.*

A flash of hot-pink hair caught her attention. *Ah ha!*

"Jamie!" she called out, while slipping through the crowd to the front of the second-tier bleachers.

Beth knew him from the non-theatre-major Musical course she took last year. While she never became fast-friends with anyone from her class, because of the nature of the work – putting on a Review together – they had bonded on another level.

"Jamie!" she called again.

He turned, a confused but curious look molding his features. When he caught sight of Beth, he flashed her one of his spectacular grins. The second she was within arm's distance, Jamie scooped her up into a hug and twirled her into the group. The familiar jolt crashed through her body with the invasion of her personal space, yet she couldn't help but laugh.

"Put me down you big oaf."

"If you insist."

Beth tried to get a buffer between them, but he wrapped an arm around her shoulders as if they were long-lost buds. She'd endured this many times, and only needed to build up her tolerance levels again.

"Did you just arrive?" Kim asked, braiding and re-braiding a wisp of her long brown hair.

"Yeah. You guys been here long?"

"Over an hour." Tank sighed. Beth smiled in sympathy, even as some faraway place in her brain shook its head and snickered at the petite girl's nickname. Their prof/director had told her to "think like a tank" during the second-last rehearsal. Well, she didn't just think like one, she'd careened into Jamie, a guy the size of a stocky football player, and sent both of them sprawling!

"What have you heard? Anything?"

"Nothing," Tank said.

"Every twenty minutes they come over the loud speakers and assure us that everything is under control and to remain calm until they learn more," Kim said.

"Okay, but what's the word? Surely you've heard something?" Beth asked.

"Wiz texted me ten minutes ago – he's visiting his Gran today – said even the radio stations are being evasive. The only speculation that's happening is based on which police units have been called in and which emergency procedures have been put in place."

"And?"

"And, the threat is 'viable and immediate'. The crews on the scene suggest it's some kind of terrorism but no one is confirming anything."

"Shit. Why aren't they just getting everyone away from here? Why box us up in the stadium?" Beth asked.

Jamie ran his fingertips over the buzz on either side of his spiked, hot pink mane. "Something about not inciting panic and there being a timeline. It must be short though, otherwise we wouldn't still be here."

Beth let the conversation naturally flow away from the tension of the moment and back to the new club everyone was hoping to check out later tonight. Clearly, they either thought the police had everything under control or believed it was a false alarm.

She wasn't going to get much more out of them, and likely only rumour about why they were being so calm about all of this. *Plan B's mostly a bust.* Beth glanced down to the field again, locking onto her last chance for definitive answers and proving Jeremy wrong.

Beth slipped out of Jamie's grasp and backed away.

"Hey, what's doin'?" His confused look stabbed at her heart, not wanting to disappoint him or herself. But she knew from experience she didn't really fit there.

"Gotta find out what's going on. Chase down another lead."

He tilted his chin up in salute, then turned back to the group. Even as Beth walked away, the ache of longing pierced across an invisible thread between them. This group was the closest she'd gotten to feeling needed. *Too bad we're worlds apart.*

At the front of the tier, Beth leaned over to assess the

field below: two officers by the main access, clumps of older students around the edges, and staff and faculty grouped by discipline toward the middle of the field. *Okay, I can do this.*

As she made her way to the lower level, Beth kept an eye out for Jeremy's contact. She hadn't texted Jeremy the signal yet, but there could only be so many black women with crimson highlights. Still, no joy on that front as Beth swallowed butterflies before passing the officers on her way out to the field. Several paces away from them, she hesitated and scanned the ads along the boards to gain her bearings. *Ah ha! The old Coke ad with the polar bear.* She walked toward the group of Soc-TA's and office staff.

But her steps slowed the closer she got. *What am I doing? I can't just breeze over there and ask outright if they know what's going on. I need an angle... but I can't lie either. Shit!*

Beth's frazzled state must have been splattered across her face because she didn't need to say anything after all. The second Rachel caught sight of her, she pulled Beth into a hug. And boy, did Beth need it. Now, that's not to say Jamie's hug wasn't appreciated, but this was a mom hug – a favourite aunt who never judges you, hug. From day one, Rachel met every student enrolled in Sociology. But she was so much more than the Chair's Executive Assistant, she was the buffer between the profs and the students, and she never forgot you. At least, that was Beth's experience.

"Oh, Elspeth. How are you doin', love?" She held Beth out at arm's length.

"Worried."

"I can see that." Rachel didn't ask where Beth's friends were or try to slough her off to finish whatever conversation she'd had with her colleagues. Beth's well-being always came first, and as much as Beth wished she were special, and Rachel only enveloped her heart around one student, Beth knew this was just who Rachel was – and she was good with that.

Beth sighed. "I'm concerned about my new friend. I don't think he can get here on his own." Rachel didn't move a muscle or imply anything about Beth's "friend" being male.

"Do you know where he is? Surely the police will find him and escort him."

"Maybe. I hope so. He's blind."

Something flashed across her eyes, and it wasn't a passing cloud in the distance.

"Jeremy's being difficult, is he?"

Beth shouldn't have been surprised that the faculty knew about Jeremy. "Stubborn, yes. Please tell me I don't have anything to worry about."

*Buzz her again. Backtracking down from 3ʳᵈ tier now,* Beth texted Jeremy. She liked his print-to-speech software. The tech's voice nagged well.

"For Christ's sake!" a gravelly, yet feminine voice cursed. Beth shot up onto her tiptoes and followed the holler to a shock of red hair whipping out of the stairwell, and watched the side of an ebony fist smacking the concrete wall. Beth dropped back down and squeezed through the circles of friends standing on the walkway between the back row of seats and the main structure.

A black heel-spike flew through the air. A bunch of students ducked and called out. As Beth reached the outer wall, she watched the girl break off the matching heel and chuck it, too, before sliding a cell into her purse. She straightened her rather tight, black, sheened skirt only to have it slide from her knees to her thighs again. She looked up.

Beth gasped. "Shaunika?"

"Who's askin'?" The tall, dark-skinned beauty who'd left Jeremy's dorm room not six days ago stared right at her, unseeing.

"Beth. Jeremy's friend."

She squinted. "I've never seen you before."

The memory of Beth sliding out of the very elevator Shaunika had slipped into that Monday afternoon also brought with it proof of Wayne's innocence.

"You stole his vial."

Shaunika blanched a sickly-grey, "I– I– What?"

"The last time you visited Jeremy on whatever tryst-bender he was on, I saw you walk into the elevator with a blue vial. His Chem experiment."

"Tryst?" She recoiled then regained some colour. "He's my math tutor."

"What? Then why were you stealing from him?"

Shaunika waved her hand in front of her face and closed her eyes briefly as if swatting the question aside. "Look. He said you needed my help to get outta here, right? I do that, you don't mention the vial. Kay?"

Beth crossed her arms. "No. You help me get out of

here, like you promised Jeremy, and you tell me why you stole his project."

"What's the big deal? It didn't even work."

Beth tilted her head and quirked an eyebrow. Shaunika mirrored Beth's stance and crossed her arms, too. Beth broke her own comfort bubble by stepping inside Shaunika's. The model was half-a-head taller than Beth, but had her back against the wall. As the dark girl's gaze slid back and forth trying to assess an escape, she drew a sharp breath and then grabbed Beth's arm. In a flash, she'd pulled Elspeth into a nearby washroom. Shaunika pushed on each stall then swung back and locked the main door.

"I didn't want to take it. Nothing happened. Jeremy's been good to me." *I'll bet he has.* "I actually passed. Got a C on my last test."

"Why did you steal it, then?" Beth leaned her glutes and palms against the edge of the sink counter, waiting.

"Because my boyfriend asked me to. But like I said, nothing happened. It was a dud. I refused to do it again. Caused some tension but we patched it up."

Beth closed her eyes and let her head droop back against her neck, then looked over at Shaunika. "Who's your boyfriend?"

"Doesn't matter."

"Yeah, it does."

"No. Deal was I'd take you to the old tunnel, get you back out. Now *that*, I can do." She inclined her head and nodded toward the door. Beth followed Shaunika out and down the stairs toward the basement.

"How do you know about the tunnels?"

"Jeremy wanted to come to the last game. It was after

one of our sessions. He showed me. I met– we met up with friends once we got here."

"Does it connect to the other tunnels?"

"I don't think so. It'll take you over to the covered grandstand behind the plaza." She turned to push open the door, then froze. As she looked through the tempered glass her gaze darted about before she pulled back and flattened herself against the wall, almost crashing into Beth. Shaunika held a finger to her lips and whispered in Beth's ear, "Guard."

Beth allowed her eyes to widen in question.

Shaunika leaned back in. "I got this. You just be ready," she breathed, then pushed off from the wall and stumbled through the basement door from the stairwell.

"Oh! Thank God!" She limped toward the stadium guard: male, and not an officer.

"Are you all right, Miss?"

"No! I took a turn down the stairs, lost my heels, and twisted my ankle. Can you help me?"

"The First Aid station is on the next floor up." He turned toward the stairwell door.

Shaunika wailed, "Oh! Don't make me climb back up those. Surely you've got an elevator…" Beth just stared in amazement as the guy thought nothing of leaving his post to help a beautiful woman in need. Shaunika draped her arm over his shoulders and hobbled beside him, off to find the elevator. The instant they were out of sight, Beth snuck through the heavy metal door into the basement and dashed across the hall to the tunnel door – her heart hammering. She yanked the handle–

*Fuck!*

## MASTERMIND

Beth pulled the handle again and again. Then, she turned and ran – back through the basement door and up the concrete stairwell to the main floor. The crush of people at the top made it difficult to squeeze onto the concourse.

"Excuse me. Excuse me – pardon me."

A strong voice blasted over the PA system, causing Beth to nearly jump out of her skin. "Thank you for remaining calm. The police are doing everything they can at this time…" The same message the theatre group said they'd been broadcasting every twenty minutes.

*I have to get out of here.*

Beth glanced up at the signs looking for the First Aid booth. Two access coves ahead, she spotted it. A hand clamped down on her shoulder. Beth's stomach bottomed-out and her knees buckled.

"Whoa, there. Are you all right?" an officer asked as she slowly turned Beth around. "The way you barrelled out of that stairwell, I thought you were being chased."

"N– No. Sorry. My friend fell and a security guard is bringing her to First Aid." Beth watched as the cop narrowed her eyes slightly with an unasked question. "Service elevator was too small to fit all of us. So I ran." *God, I hope she's not familiar with this place.* Beth's heart beat so loud, she could hear it in her ears.

"First Aid's over there." She pointed. "Slow down, okay? We don't want any more accidents." Beth nodded vigorously, then slower, before stepping away from the officer. She could feel the weight of the woman's stare as she took care to manoeuvre between people this time, instead of pushing and shoving and causing potential havoc. *Smarten up, Beth. You're not gonna get out of here by drawing attention to yourself. Think!*

And yet, because she chose to glance over her shoulder one last time, Beth walked right into Shaunika on her way out of First Aid.

"What the hell, girl?"

This time, Beth took Shaunika by the arm and steered her to a pair of bleacher seats away from most of the crowds. Beth pulled the beauty down onto the collapsible chair beside her.

"It was locked."

"So? Why didn't you pick it?"

"What? I don't know how to do that. Do you?"

"No. But if you're planning on sneaking around, I figured you had the skill-set."

Beth dropped her head into her hands and groaned. "I have to get out of here. Jeremy's waiting for me. I– I–" But she couldn't tell a stranger, one who stole an early attempt at the experiment no less, the reason why.

"I promised Jeremy I'd get you out of here. I plan to do that."

"How?" Beth looked up as she gripped her knees and stared out at the half-empty field.

"Workin' on it."

They both just sat and looked straight ahead. Beth's brain refused to calculate, to make the necessary connections to get out of here. She could only hope Shaunika's problem-solving street-skills were better than her book ones. Just as a custodian wandered by on the far side of the bleachers, picking up bits of garbage with a pointed jabber, Shaunika gripped Beth's wrist.

"I got it."

"Oww. What? You got what? My bones? I feel that, very distinct–"

"Would you listen already? I'm surprised Jeremy puts up with you." Beth recoiled at the verbal slap. "We're gonna send you out exactly the same way you came in."

❦

B eth found herself back in the washroom, door locked, getting poked and prodded by Black Beauty. She'd been forbidden to look at her watch after the first three times caused Shaunika to smudge the make-up.

"Hold still, girl. Haven't you ever done this before?"

Beth smacked Shaunika's hand away from her face. "Yes. Just not often."

Shaunika grabbed Beth's chin and jerked her head back into position as she added yet more smoky-grey eyeshadow in places other than over her eyes.

"All right, then." She snapped her compact shut and swept the rest of her makeup into her tiny purse. Beth marvelled at its hidden-depths. "Take a look."

Beth slowly turned toward the mirror and stared open-mouthed at her reflection. "Oh my God, Shaunika, you did it." Beth turned back and, channelling Jamie's exuberance, gave the model a hug.

"Okay, okay. Okay!" She shook Beth off and straightened her outfit before heading for the door.

"Wait." Beth grabbed her arm. "Remember your promise," she said, and held Shaunika's gaze with as heavy a stare as she had in her.

"Don't you worry. *I* keep my promises," she said, then unlocked the door and left.

Beth waited the agreed-upon ten minutes, hoping no one else came through the door. *Thank God for small miracles.* She made a sharp right turn and pushed the garbage receptacle toward the ramp and right back out the way she came – just like Shaunika said.

Fewer people walked the halls on the way in now, making it relatively easy to manoeuvre the large bin. But as the double-wide doors opened, a group of officers dressed all in black stood right outside. Bold white letters, S-I-U, stood out on both the front and back of their uniforms. Their guns, Tasers, and two-way radios pulled her gaze. The bin bounced over the threshold and every officer turned to look at her.

*Oh shit, oh shit, oh shit!* She averted her eyes, but one cop followed Beth as she turned to avoid the group.

"Hold up there," he said, tilting his head slightly. Beth moved to the far side, placing the bin between them, and pulled the pointed garbage grabber from inside. He glanced at the tan uniform Shanika insisted Beth "borrow". His gaze lingered over the rolled cuffs and baggy ripples of extra fabric around her middle. She held her breath.

He looked inside the bin. Empty except for a stash of black garbage bags. He stared at Beth far longer than necessary.

"Hey, Bill! Come on. The South Sweep's just checked in clean. Let's move."

The officer gave Beth a near imperceptible nod, then turned and marched off with his team. Beth nearly peed her pants as she stifled a manic laugh, stabbed a crumpled page and three wrappers from the grass, and pushed the bin as far away from Police Grand Central as possible. At the back entrance, she spied another guard – not a cop. Backtracking to the side of the large building, she shimmied out of the uniform, left it draped over the edge of the bin, and ran. She tried to tell herself not to, but it happened anyway.

Beth staggered toward the empty bench in the parkette behind the plaza – Jeremy was nowhere in sight. *They found him! I'm too late!* Her legs wobbled. She gripped the back of the bench as a sob escaped past her lips. The scrape of shoes on asphalt made her head jerk up as a black-clad officer walked past the corner of the building. The breeze picked up, cutting right through her sweater. Shaunika had kept Beth's jacket during the costume change.

A large hand gripped her shoulder and hauled her into the bushes. Her heart leapt up into her throat, stopping her from screaming – that, and Jeremy's hushed voice.

"You're sure? You've tried?" He pulled her down to the woodchipped ground. If these hadn't been evergreens, she would have laughed at the absurdity of hiding in plain sight. As it was, the thick, cloying scent of cedar made her cough into her sleeve.

"Yeah, we'll connect later. See ya." Jeremy disconnected his call and rubbed a free hand over his face. "That was Moxie. He's off campus with his sister."

"You're calling the team?"

"Every one."

"What did you find?" Beth asked, unsure if he'd lie to her or not.

"You first. You okay? You were gone awhile." He reached out and found her arms again. "Where's your jacket."

"Long story. Tunnel was locked, had to find another way out." Beth sighed, trying to loosen some of the tension from her body, but the chill air and the nearness of that cop kept her on edge.

"What did you learn?" he asked.

"Nothing but rumour and speculation at first. Then I found the Sociology Dean's Assistant and she told me everything the staff had been given."

"And?"

"And you were right. It's a bomb threat. The cops are keeping everyone at the stadium because apparently it could go off at any time. The information they gathered is under suspect but they believe it's an inside job. They still can't confirm if this is a hoax or not, but they're treating it as real. What did you find?"

"Everyone's accounted for except–"

Beth's phone buzzed. She pulled it from her back pocket. Shaunika, as promised, with a one-word text.

*Wayne.*

"Wayne," Jeremy said.

Beth dropped her cell in her lap and grabbed Jeremy's hands. He jolted slightly and tried to look toward her face, his eyes vainly searching for something in the depths of their shadows to lock onto.

"You have to turn yourself in."

"Elle, you kn–"

"No, Jeremy. Listen to me. You can tell them about Wayne, show them you're not the one they're looking for, and help them find this thing before it goes off."

Jeremy dropped his phone, too, and turned his hands to grasp hers back. "I can't do that."

"Yes. Yes, you can."

Jeremy pulled her toward him and gingerly touched foreheads. "Wayne is a mastermind. He gets people to do things they wouldn't normally," he said.

Beth thought of Shaunika and the vial.

"He will have manipulated the evidence. And if I can't make this bomb disappear before it's found, or God-forbid goes off, then everyone will know I turned a harmless theoretical assignment into a practical nightmare and I'll lose everything. My Masters' prof, my diploma, my clean record... even my freedom. Because I *will* get charged and they won't care that I'm blind or was set up to take the fall. I shouldn't have made the damn thing in the first place. Beth…"

It was difficult to breathe. His point, his forehead, his hands, her heart—

"…will you be my eyes? Will you help me find the bomb?"

"Yes."

## CRYPTIC WORDS

Beth's grip fell from Jeremy's elbow for the fourth time. She leaned away from him around yet another building corner. They headed south, based on her intel about where the cops had already been. Her choice, not his. He had to trust they were headed in the right direction. Jeremy had convinced her to sneak back through the tunnel, but from there, they wended their way outside toward the Science Library. The chill of the fall afternoon cut through his sweater, but the heat he generated from jogging and the adrenaline from fear numbed him. Still, she had to stop abandoning him.

"Ahum–"

"Shhh."

The air current changed as she waved her hand at him. He grabbed her arm on the next upswing. She tensed but didn't pull away. Switching his grip, Jeremy caught her hand and held it. Beth squeezed an apology then entwined her fingers through his. A strange ache filled his chest, something he hadn't experienced in a long time – not since high school.

"Okay. Come on." She tugged forward and he followed. They were close to the library, but because they'd gone all clandestine he was unfamiliar with the path Beth chose, and her stride-lengths threw off his counts.

"Wall. Left," she whispered. He ran his free hand over the brickwork until she pulled him to a crouch. "We're here. Front door's probably locked. This is the back." Beth guided his hand. "These windows lead into the basement."

The coolness of the glass under his fingers cued Jeremy to the window, but the angle was off. He ran his fingers along the glass until he found the frame.

"It's open!" he whispered. "Is it big enough to crawl through?"

"Yeah. They upgraded the lower-level windows my first year. I had to bypass construction on the way to Psych 101. Pain in the ass."

"I remember that." His fingers slipped under the open frame, grazing a metal mesh. "Screen."

The grind of Beth shifting her feet over gravel travelled easily to Jeremy's hearing. Her knee bumped his on its way to the ground. The dark, undefined shadow before him lowered as she leaned toward the opening.

"If I can turn the plastic clips far enough, it should release the screen. There's six of them. One in each corner and two parallel in the middle."

"How are you going to do that? Do you have a nail file in your purse?"

"I don't carry a purse." The sweep of her sweater told

him she reached back, probably to her jeans pocket. "I do have a wallet and several plastic cards."

"You've got a credit card?"

"Bank card. But I'm not going to chance wrecking that." He heard her shuffle through several pieces of plastic then slide her wallet back again. "Emergency Auto Service Card."

"Well, aren't you Nancy Drew." Jeremy shifted and sat with his back against the wall as Beth grunted.

"It won't budge," she said.

"What?"

"The window. It's on a crank-system. I can't force it." Suddenly her centre of gravity got a hell of lot lower. "I can get it."

Her card scraped and flipped as she got up under the frame to work on turning the latches from the outside. The card flicked out of the slot as she breathed deeply again and again, possibly to keep from swearing or yelling in frustration. A scattering of stones made Jeremy jerk his head to the side.

"Wait," he whispered

"What?"

"Someone's near."

"Shit." She struggled out from under the window. "Ahh!" She yelped, then whined as she curled in on herself.

"What happened?"

She inhaled a shaky breath. "Sliced my hand on the frame."

Feet crunched on gravel. "Someone's coming."

"From where?"

"The way we came." He gave a vague motion by his

right ear. Beth grabbed the shoulder of his sweater, yanking him up and in the opposite direction, around the far side of the library. She flattened him with an arm against the wall and waited. Jeremy willed his heart to stop pounding so he could hear better.

Beth crept to the corner. She took a deep breath and he followed the rustle of her clothes as she peered around the side before snaking back to him even closer – shoulder to shoulder, hip to hip. Her lips brushed his ear. He squeezed his eyelids shut and bit his tongue to clear his mind.

"Stay here."

And then she was gone. He barely heard her slip away before he smacked the back of his head against the brick and sighed. *I hate it when she does that.* Every time she'd let go of his elbow it was like she suddenly disappeared and he was all alone, stranded. Being all covert and subtle, meant it didn't take much to lose her, especially when the wind picked up and stole her sound. It was doubly worse when it made his teeth chatter. Jeremy tried to shake off the full-body grip that came with the doubt.

Then she was back.

"A single scout." Her breath warmed his cheek. "Walked past the front and kept going." The strained edge to her voice said more about the pain she hid than it did her feelings about the situation.

"How bad is your hand?" he asked, as she slipped past him and back down to her knees.

She hesitated longer than he liked. "I'll clean it up when we get inside." And she went back to Nancy Drew-ing the screen.

Jeremy's insides cramped in indignation. "Let me help."

"You– can't– see," she grunted as she worked. His arm twitched as he held his fist back from punching the wall. She'd never spoken to him like that before.

"No shit. I can still help." He crouched down next to her, ran his hand down her lower back to her jeans pocket. She shuddered – from the cold?

"What are you doing?" She turned to him and snatched her wallet back.

"Getting my own card. It'll go faster if you let me help."

"But–"

"Beth. I can help."

She sighed, flipped open the leather holder, and slid a piece of plastic from inside. "Here." She placed it in his hand. A drop of something damp moistened the base of his palm. "Library card."

He heard the trace of a smile in her voice. Apt, considering where they were breaking into. She shifted, likely to put her wallet away again and went back to work on the middle latches. Jeremy wiped his palm on the side of his jeans, aware her hand was worse off than she let on. He found the edge of the window and traced it until the screen revealed the small slots Beth was already flicking her card at again.

He slid the corner of the plastic into the notch and wiggled it until it shifted around. When he couldn't work it any more, he angled down and loosened the next one.

"Okay. That oughta do it," she whispered. "Move back."

Jeremy leaned away as he heard Beth shove the screen. It creaked but didn't budge – at least not that he noticed. He felt her get back down on her stomach and reach under the awning-style glass of the window. The screen screeched with a springing rebound that made him think she used her fist. It clattered down inside. Then came the definitive squeak of the crank turning and the window opening wider.

"There's computers on the table below. I'll slide in first and then guide you."

Jeremy nodded, holding her library card out. She plucked it from his fingers. The scrape of fabric against metal told him she inched her way inside, over the lintel.

"Okay. Get on your stomach and slowly aim your legs toward me. I mean, my voice." She supported Jeremy's ankles as he wiggled backward through the opening, feet out in a reverse Superman, and then lowered his suspended feet to the table. His shoes bumped either side of a monitor.

The table groaned. The soles of her shoes scraped the edge of the table as she jumped to the floor. The grinding of chair legs on low-pile carpet made him hesitate.

"Here." She held his hips and tugged him backward. Hands resting on the wall under the window, he raised one leg up a bit. Beth ran her hand down his thigh, helping position the limb so his foot touched the seat of the chair. He pushed back off the wall, and both of Beth's hands returned to his hips as he used his arms to keep balance, until blissfully flat-footed on the floor.

"Where to?" Beth asked, a hint of a tremor in her voice. They were looking for a bomb after all, not some insignificant, first year assignment. *Shouldn't even have been a final year assignment.*

"Third floor."

Beth remembered to interlock her fingers with Jeremy's. A warm calm spread through him as she led him up the stairs, the elevators a bust since they'd been turned off.

"Wait. Your other hand. Bring us to the main counter."

"It can wait."

"No, it can't. You're bleeding. There should be a medical kit by the firehose next to the office door."

She let go of his hand and in the next moment metal scraped Formica before the case's clasps snapped open. He listened as she unwound the roll of gauze and picked up the scissors.

"Take it into the washroom. You should at least rinse it out before using the rubbing alcohol."

"Yes, doctor." The words were playful but the tightness to her vocal chords said she was mad at him. He sighed as the washroom door banged open. *What did I do now? This is why you don't date, Jeremy. Women are too unpredictable.*

In no time, Beth returned, the scissors clattered back into the case, and she had it back up on the wall before he could think to ask her how deep the cut was. She clasped his elbow, not his hand, her grip tighter than necessary.

At the top of the stairs to the third floor, surety flowed through him, and, without thinking, he pulled away from her and took the lead. Jeremy felt the heat of her body as she followed close behind.

He was here often enough that the head librarian knew

not to change the layout of the tables and chairs without first giving Jeremy significant forewarning. It only took a knee-crack against a wooden chair once, in second year, to solidify his point with the staff about random floorplan changes – and he'd even had his cane with him at the time.

Jeremy brushed his fingertips on each path marker (chair, table, pillar, etcetera) as he made his way over to the microfiche counter... and around to the office. Beth followed, but a little farther behind this time. He walked over to the storage room and turned the handle.

"Locked," he said.

"So, it's not in there?"

"No, it just means whoever was last on shift followed protocol. We have to find the keys."

Beth bent near the lock. "It's a special one – round." She stood up. "Wouldn't it still be with the last person who used it?"

"No. Not–"

"Protocol?" she finished. "And how is it you know so much about the inner workings of the Science Library?"

A hot flush crept up his cheeks.

"You've gotta be kidding me." She turned and went back out to the main desk, yanking open counter doors and drawers.

He couldn't read her. One minute her touch said one thing and the next, her voice said something completely different. She knew he wasn't a saint. Jeremy shook his head then checked out the two desks in the office. He found the key hanging at the back of the bottom drawer.

"Got it!"

Beth shuffled to the doorframe. He returned to the

storage door and unlocked it. She came up beside him and looked over his shoulder.

"I don't see a bomb."

"The cops would have found it if he'd left it out in the open." Jeremy walked in past two sets of metal drawer-shelves which he knew were packed solid with microfilm boxes. After five strides, he reached his arms out and bumped his knuckles against an old wooden podium. He smiled, remembering the acrobatics Hannah enticed him to try – but the memory of that tryst vanished when the scent of clean soap and mint wafted past him, and the length of Beth's body flattened against the back of his.

Jeremy shoved the podium aside and knelt down.

Beth gasped, "Is that what I think it is?"

Jeremy ran his hand over the linoleum-tile flooring until his fingers hooked under a latch. He doubted Wayne would have rigged the panel to the bomb but…

"Maybe you should go downstairs, just in case."

"Call the cops, Jeremy. Let them handle this – Christ! It's their job."

"Go downstairs, Beth."

"No. Call them."

He shook his head, squared his shoulders, and heaved up on the latch.

Beth shrieked.

Jeremy cringed.

Nothing blew up.

He forced the panel all the way back and stared at the shadows that had plagued his sight since he was ten. "What do you see?"

Beth shuffled forward and leaned over him, her hair brushing past his cheek. Then, she punched him.

"Nothing," she growled, and hit him with the flats of her hands, assaulting his body with blow after blow. That's when she sobbed. Jeremy stood up and turned in one swift motion, gathering her into his arms, holding her tight. The sides of her fists pushed into his chest even as her tears soaked the front of his sweater.

He rested his cheek against the top of Beth's head and pushed back the memory of Wayne's tight, forced laughter when he'd found Jeremy and Hannah half-naked in that very storage room. It wasn't until Wayne had spoken that Jeremy realized Hannah hadn't been a prize in their game after all – he'd truly liked her. Unfortunately, that wasn't the only place Jeremy needed to look for the bomb, just as it wasn't the only time in the past three years Jeremy had gotten between Wayne and what he wanted.

## LAB RAT

**B**eth buried her nose into the hollow of Jeremy's collarbone and breathed in Irish Spring laced with sweat – better than BBQ. But the longer she remained curled inside his arms, the faster her thoughts spun. *Why can't he trust the system? What's he trying to prove? Did we really just avoid being blown up? Why here? Was it something to do with that look on his face earlier? Why do I bother?* And that's what it all boiled down to… why *did* Beth give Jeremy the time of day? Why did she agree to his asinine plan? Certainly not to keep her sanity. She'd like to believe it was to help save lives, but the campus had been evacuated – no one was going to get hurt.

Except Jeremy.

He would either have gone looking for that damn bomb on his own or allowed himself to become the scapegoat for Wayne's twisted sense of justice. And as freaked out as Beth was, she knew better than to ask Jeremy, again, to give up on this foolishness. School was his life. *Seven years for God's sake, and looking to take his Masters.*

Beth allowed herself to inhale Jeremy's scent and hold it in her lungs just one last time before pulling away and wiping her eyes. She breathed through the strange ache in her chest that triggered at the stupidest of times, and placed her hands on her hips.

"What was your north option again?" she asked, referring to his initial breakdown of possible bomb locations.

"The lab." His voice hitched. He cleared his throat and swallowed. Beth watched his Adam's apple jump as he fumbled for something to do with his now vacant arms.

Beth kept her voice hard, focused. "That's basically on the boarder between the south portion of campus and the more northerly buildings, right?"

"Yeah."

"Good. Maybe we won't run into anyone. Maybe the team of cops, doing their job by the way, will be over in the west quadrant by now." *And have found the bomb.*

"There's a tunnel access in the basement I've used before. It should keep us out of sight."

*Great, yet another tunnel.*

**B**eth didn't bother to hold his hand this time, Jeremy knew where he was going – but that didn't mean some crazy part of her didn't want to. They were friends, that was it. To hell with her thesis. She had to believe there was something between them for this trust thing to work.

He didn't date girls like her and she didn't think about guys like him.

Except she did.

Well, not other guys. Just him. A split-second before she'd pushed him away the first time he'd held her face, she'd almost done the opposite. And that's what scared her more than thinking he was coming on to her. Then, when she found out he was blind, and making a pass at her hadn't even crossed his mind… she was mortified. She was supposed to be the "good girl". All her cousins were either "living in sin" or had kids before they got married. One never even bothered to tell the father. She didn't fall for hunky Hollywood stars – why waste her time? She didn't drool over the hot jocks or sexy theatre students – what was the point? She was just plain Beth and always would be.

Jeremy stopped moving and she bumped into him.

"Oh, sorry," Beth mumbled.

"Do you mind checking to see if the coast is clear?"

"Right."

Beth cleared her head and focused on the weight of the old door instead of her buzzing thoughts. She didn't want to yank so hard as to potentially reveal to someone on the other side they were there, but she had to pull hard enough to crack the door open the width of her eyeball.

She tugged and the door didn't budge.

"Shit," she whispered. Jeremy heard but didn't say anything. Beth tried again, this time with a little more pizazz on the backswing. It popped open with a whomp. She almost let go and ran. Almost. Her heart thundered in her ears and screamed at her to end this. Instead, Beth took a shaky breath, reminded herself of the promise she'd made, and peered through the crack.

"The coast is clear." She shifted to open the door the rest of the way.

"Wait."

"What? Why?"

"Take a second to listen."

She stared at Jeremy with her confused, are-you-serious look until she remembered he couldn't see her, so what was the point? Beth rested her ear against the edge of the door and the metal frame, and listened.

"Still nothing," she said.

Jeremy nodded. Beth yanked the door open the rest of the way and followed him in. She caught herself watching him. His air of confidence belied the minimized toe sweep when he got near the base of the stairs. The natural way his arm swept out in an arc before his hand found the railing added to his swagger. And, the relaxed set of his shoulders, his whole posture for that matter, exuded an easy competence and trust in himself and the environment around him. It was no wonder she hadn't picked up on the other cues – she'd wanted to see him a certain way, and so she had. Beth had been so convinced her thesis was right, she'd blocked everything else from consideration – she hadn't allowed herself to properly assess each of their meetings with an open mind.

She reeled with information overload. Even Jeremy had said she was the first person his tactics had worked on. It was an act. A role he played. *Am I that gullible or does that make me too trusting? I didn't question anything. Like Wayne. I never questioned his dedication to their friendship.*

Barking erupted when they reached the top of the stairs. Beth whipped her head toward the sound and her knees nearly buckled.

"Jeremy!" A man stood backlit by a break in the clouds as the sun cast him in shadow by the window at the end of the hall.

"What? The dogs?"

"The man." Her throat constricted the words. Part of her felt the giddiness of relief, they'd been caught. No more sneaking around. Part of her coiled tighter than she ever thought possible.

He didn't move.

*It's Wayne! He's waiting for Jeremy! Shit, shit, shit.* Beth let out an involuntary squeak.

"By the window?"

Beth grabbed Jeremy's arm and held on tight. But he loosened her fingers and stepped forward. He held a hand in the sunshine haloing around the figure, and wiggled his fingers as if playing with the light and heat. "That's just Mr. Spock. Did he startle you?"

And then the clouds ate the sun and the dark outline became a cardboard cut out of Leonard Nimoy in his most famous role.

"It's our nod to Big Bang Theory. Have you seen it? The show."

A strange half-laugh, half-shriek escaped her throat as she thought of the group of geniuses the TV show revolved around, and how this simple cut-out would not only inspire the students studying to become scientists, but appeal to the "logical" geeky-fun side of them. *Still, I nearly shit my pants.* Beth turned away from Spock and headed down the corridor on the first level.

"Which lab?"

Jeremy hurried after. "The last one." He slipped past her and opened the door. "It won't be anywhere obvious. The cops will have already checked in here."

"So, where is un-obvious enough for Wayne to trick a sniffer dog?"

Jeremy walked over to a locked metal cabinet and stared at it only a hand's breath from his nose, hands on hips. "Their dogs are useless."

"How's that now?" Beth asked, as she looked around the room filled with tall work tables, gas lines, and mini-sinks that reminded her of grade ten science on steroids.

"The laser cooling technique slows the atoms down enough that the odour is no longer detectable."

"But… it won't stay cold or slow forever. It will warm up again and – smell?"

"Yes. And that's when Wayne will have triggered it to explode. That's why there's a limited amount of time for us to find it."

"Once the atoms speed up again they'll explode?"

"No. But he's got the catalyst and if he's triggered the hammer, or whatever, to spark ignition it'll either be on a timer he's rigged it to when he thinks the bomb will become detectable, or he's set up a sensor so that it doesn't explode too soon. Obviously, Wayne has his own genius."

"I wouldn't call it that. Why on earth would you take this from theoretical to practical, Jeremy? And in your *dorm room* while we were having coffee no less!" She hauled off and punched him in the shoulder again.

"Hey! Ow! What are you doing? It would have been fine. As soon as I discovered the rate at which the atoms could be slowed and still combust with an energy output–"

"You're talking gibberish. Me speak-a no chemistry. Again, I ask, why even do this in the first place? It's insane." Beth stalked off to pace around the nearest lab table. Jeremy held the lock for the cabinet in one hand, the other rubbed his bruised shoulder.

"Fossil fuels are ancient tech." She heard the hint of a smile in his voice at the bad pun. "There's only so much renewable resources can do. We've dabbled in ethanol, fuel from corn, but there's no way we could manufacture enough of the grain to truly make it a viable alternative. My project looks at taking relatively common, renewable and man-made substances, and using them as a fuel source for a combustible engine. But you smelled the rotten eggs when I ignited that drop of fuel – no one is going to want to drive around having their car smell like ass. They already complain about the veggie oil fuels smelling like French Fries. So, it had to be odourless. But you can't remove odour from a substance without changing the chemical makeup."

"The point, Jeremy? What's the point?"

"The point is, I had to know for sure if my theory would work. I had to be chosen by Professor Young over all the competition. And I did it... at least on a small scale. The interior makeup of the engine that would use this fuel would be drastically different than what's out there, *and* require a six-point laser cooling–"

Beth cleared her throat. "Ahem."

"So, the dogs wouldn't smell my experiment until moments before it exploded – when the cooling wore off enough to allow detection of the odour again. Like I said, they're useless. I have to find this thing. Can you pick a lock?"

"You're the second person who's asked me that today."

"I take it that's a no?"

"Yeah, that's a no. I'm not some all-knowing street thug."

"I could do it when I was eight."

"Eight?"

"I liked to think I was a detective."

"But you can't now."

"Nope. Need to see. At least, for the kind of lock work I did back then. We have to get this open."

"What's in the cabinet?"

"Chemicals."

"And you think the cops wouldn't have checked it?"

"It's what's behind them I don't think they would've checked."

Beth knelt down in front of the lock, shoving Jeremy over a step, and looked at the key opening. She pulled out her smartphone, got online, and searched *How to Pick a Key Lock.*

"Bingo. I'll need two paper clips and a pair of pliers. Is there a flashlight around? It's kinda dark in here."

Once she and Jeremy located the necessary tools, it took maybe ten minutes to pop the lock. But after the echo of the lock-base hitting the metal cabinet, both she and Jeremy froze. The silence stretched out between them like two rafts being separated by waves on the ocean. Beth just couldn't make herself remove the dangling, open lock from the door. It was one of those unspoken barriers her brain wouldn't let her cross. Just as Jeremy should have had a barrier telling him not to make his project a reality. Masters or no, blind or no, it was one of those things you just didn't do.

"Why here?" she asked.

The break in the heavy silence jolted him into action. He removed the lock, opened the cabinet, and started taking out various jars, containers, and cans plastered with flammable and poison symbols... even a few bio-hazard WHMIS icons. Here she was, a student of humanity – a people watcher and analyzer – and she had absolutely no idea what made him tick. Or why she seemed to be attracted to him – not that she'd ever admit that out loud.

"Jeremy, why would Wayne hide the bomb here? What's the significance?"

He remained quiet until the entire middle shelf was empty, and then he pointed inside. Beth tilted her head and looked in.

*A secret compartment.*

"Why am I not surprised? How did you find out about this one or should I even ask?"

"Professor Young showed me. It's where the Masters' students keep key components of experiments – for safety purposes."

"And why did she show you, a fourth year-going-on-seven, something only a Masters' student should know?"

"I impressed her."

"Something tells me there's more to this. How is Wayne involved?"

Jeremy pursed and then moved his lips around on his face as if deciding how much he should say. Beth shook her head in disbelief then stared at the small door at the back of the cabinet that clearly opened into the wall behind.

"We both approached Professor Young after her lecture. We knew we'd find her in the lab, her lab. That's when we learned she only mentored one student every two years. She made the off-hand comment that something she was working on was a *Gulliver's Travels* situation. I nodded and smiled and Wayne said *what?* So, I explained the research they were doing over at the Norwegian University of Science and Tech. A couple of students had written a blog article about the relativity of an outcome based on the size, in their case nanotechnology, of the matter being manipulated. Anyway, the article was never in any of our assigned readings but I followed the nano-rabbit down the hole one day after a particularly interesting lecture and stumbled across it."

"That's it? You read an article he hadn't."

"No. Not only had I read that article, but I understood how it pertained to the prof's research. And then, Professor Young put the nail in my coffin, so to speak, by remarking something like, 'You should be asking Jeremy to mentor you'. And then she said she'd share a post-grad secret with me."

"So, not only did you prove you were more curious than Wayne, but the prof dissed him in front of you and showed favouritism to you over him. Wow." Beth scratched her cheek. She couldn't fathom how someone could go to such an extreme – and yet, wasn't that exactly what Jeremy was doing? Sure, he was trying to stop a crisis – but for his own personal gain. Beth didn't know what to think anymore, so she didn't. She reached inside the cabinet.

"Whoa. What are you doing?"

"What you asked me to. I'm gonna see if the bomb is back there." Her fingers brushed up against a raised panel.

She ducked her head inside the cabinet and found a keypad. Her chest pulled in tight on itself, stealing her breath. *How many times can I do this? How much longer until the fuel comes to temp and primes the bomb?* But Beth didn't voice any of those questions.

"What's the code? No, wait." She pulled her head out past the echo of her voice. "How would Wayne even know about this spot if the prof only told you?"

"Let's just say Wayne wouldn't have needed to look up how to pick a lock. It's in his nature to figure this stuff out. It's 817 – the number of light years from here to Orion's Belt. Professor Young wanted us to strive for the stars and be warriors."

Beth ducked back into the middle shelf of the cabinet and punched in the code. The lock disengaged. She took a breath and pulled the safe door open.

This time, it wasn't empty.

## SUPERHERO OR SUPERVILLAIN

The hair on Jeremy's skin rose with Beth's intake of breath. *The bomb is here... now what? Shit, what have I gotten us into?* But then his ears caught the unmistakable sound of paper shifting inside the safe.

"What is it?" he asked.

"A blank piece of paper folded in half." Beth passed it to him. A number of bumps and ridges flared out beneath his fingertips as letters and numbers ignited in his mind.

"It's not blank." The lack of natural light in this room would make it difficult for her to see.

Beth snatched the sheet from Jeremy's hand. "What are you talking about?" She shifted away from him. The page snapped as if being held up for study. "There's nothing– Oh."

"Exactly."

"Is that braille? Is he sending you a message?"

Jeremy followed her voice and tugged the sheet from her hands. He spread it flat on a nearby table, and dusted his fingers across to read what Beth couldn't. It was a familiar series of formulas to be plotted on a graph. A stupid joke. He crumpled the sheet and tossed it into the lab, a snarl etched onto his usually calm face.

Beth took hold of Jeremy's elbow and turned him back toward her, closer than usual. "What is it? What did he say?"

"He's taunting me."

"How? Spill it." Tension warred with exasperation in her voice.

"The answer to each formula, plotted along with it's reciprocal onto a graph, will make the outline of a bat."

"Excuse me?"

"It's an old joke. It's the Bat Symbol from Batman. He's saying 'nana nana nana na' or 'na-na na na-na na' like a kid might before sticking out his tongue."

"Or it could be darker. Batman was a vigilante out for revenge. This could be Wayne justifying himself... making you the bad guy in all this. Oh my God. Batman is Bruce *Wayne*. This is nuts."

"Ugh," Jeremy groaned, dropping back against the side of the tall table and gripping his forehead. "He's insane." He rubbed his hands over his face and left them there as his brain searched through everything that had happened between them. Finally, one moment flickered to life in his mind's eye. "I know where it is. If this is revenge and he's taunting me, then the bomb has to be in the Strong building, on the main floor, in the two-storey multipurpose room."

"I know that space. My musical theatre class performed our final Review there last year. But it's—"

"On the east side of campus, where the cops are likely combing every inch of every building, right now."

Beth's voice held too much hope. "So then, they'll find it."

"Not if they can't see it."

"There's nowhere to hide a bomb in that room."

"Sure there is. And it's up to us to find it. Come on."

Beth shut the safe's door and then they shoved bottles and jars back into the cabinet before resetting the lock and leaving the way they came.

Just before Jeremy stepped out into the hazy sunlight at the end of the tunnel, he stopped and turned to Beth. "I don't know how to get to the Strong building from here." He held out his hand to her hoping she'd understand the peace-offering.

She didn't take it right away.

His heart to leapt when she finally did. *Come on, man. It's just Beth.* But that was how she looked at herself. He couldn't kid himself that he saw her the same way. Jeremy had no idea why she insisted on having coffee with him that first time – she knew what kind of guy he was, he pretended to be – and yet, she'd still wanted to make a connection.

The squeeze she gave his hand before taking the lead reassured the lost and hidden places within him that maybe she'd sensed who he really was all along. Just that scared fat kid wanting nothing more than a friend. But then, she pulled his arm under hers, clamping them together in a most possessive way. He smirked, feeling his body tighten in response. *God, she has no idea what a turn-on that is.* His grin faded as the subtler parts of his brain clued in to her hunched stance, short, quick steps, and shallow breathing – she was on high-alert in spy mode.

Beth altered course just enough to bring them within a copse of trees next to a walkway. Her body shifted against him every time she swung her head from side-to-side. Skirting around the sides and backs of buildings meant avoiding large metal garbage bins and decorative fencing, things Beth had to adjust for after knocking him into a few.

Then, Jeremy heard the muted jiggle of heavy gym bags, or at least the sound he associated with those objects. He pulled back on Beth's arm, stopping her from leaving the safety of the nearby brick wall. It absorbed the sun and radiated heat even as the pair of them shivered at a gust of icy wind.

Beth turned toward Jeremy. He held a finger to his lips and inclined his head toward the other side of the building. She squeezed his hand then gingerly leaned forward. Beth snapped back and moulded them both against the wall, her breathing tripled in speed. He could only assume it was a team of searchers carrying relatively heavy gear, like bullet proof vests and jackets to keep warm. That sounded a lot like guys leaving the Athletics Centre after a workout. Jeremy heard them move past the building, and then a nearly indistinct shuffling of feet made him think of the old cartoon cops shifting around in concentric circles as they checked out an open area.

Beth disengaged from the wall and walked sideways as they skirted the perimeter of the building. Jeremy was surprisingly calm. Wayne's note left him with a sense of surety, and his faith in Beth was absolute. That was until she whispered, "There's no way in."

"What? There has to be."

"No windows open, no doors unlocked, no fire escapes, and no people-sized ventilation shafts to crawl through." Sarcasm clipped her voice. "The team is sweeping the commons and systematically checking everything around the outside of the next building."

"They're getting ready to go inside. When they do, we can break a windo–"

"No."

"Excuse me?"

"I said no. It's bad enough we're disobeying an evacuation call and traipsing around campus looking for a bomb, but I'm not busting a window. I'm just not. The second we can be pinned with anything other than ignoring a direct order, we're looking at having a mark on our record. Employers look at that stuff, Jeremy. There's still nothing Wayne can do or say that isn't your word against his in this matter."

"Not true. If he tells them as a 'concerned citizen' that he saw bomb-making supplies in my dorm room, and I'm supposed to only be a theoretical chemist... well, I'm going down regardless. I'll break the window."

He dropped to a crouch, pulling out of her grip. Rocks too small to get the job done traced under his fingers until he felt a stone flowerbed edger. Using both hands, he tried to shift it from the hardened earth and paved walkway.

"Jeremy, no!" she whispered earnestly, and grabbed his shoulders. He shrugged her off, could feel her lose her balance, and fall on her ass. He yanked the stone, dirt and all, from the bed and searched for a basement window.

From her place on the ground, Beth said, as calm as if ordering dinner, "I'll scream."

Jeremy's hand tapped glass.

"You wouldn't. You promised."

"I promised to help a friend get out of a jam. Not commit a felony. I never agreed to break and enter. We're here to stop a crime, not commit one."

It wasn't so much her words as the sound of disbelief in Beth's voice that made Jeremy drop the rock. "How do we get inside then?"

"I was thinking we might use the back door."

"Back door? You said the doors are locked."

"But as we speak, the front door of the William Small Centre is being unlocked. And you of all people should know about the Boiler Room."

Jeremy's face came alive – eyes widened, smile broadened, forehead raised. The basements of both buildings were joined below the outdoor walkway by a common boiler room – a place Jeremy frequented all too often in his first and second years.

"We just need to figure out how to get inside without anyone seeing us."

Jeremy gave Beth his most devilish grin, then pulled her up from the ground and whispered in her ear.

## POKER FACE

The combination of fear, being coiled tighter than a mini-Slinky, and another injection of adrenaline from her brain added to the numbness overwhelming Beth. Not five minutes ago, a team of six trained SRU officers breached the William Small Centre looking for the bomb. Now, Beth utilized the deep shadows, gifted by an overcast sun, to hide in as she made her way to the back of the building, alone. Jeremy sat in a dark alcove at the base of the wide front steps where they met the main entrance – waiting for the signal.

Beth spotted the perfect scapegoat growing near a first-floor window. Using her sweater, pulled up over her hands like mittens, she fought to unwind the thick metal twine holding the green rubber doughnut around the young tree, using her dorm room key for leverage. The back of her sore hand throbbed with the strain. *Jeremy should have said he needed my hands, not my eyes.* But both were reality. He'd be far worse-off without her, and nowhere near as close to finding Wayne's bomb.

The metal sprang out and smacked her in the chin. She wiped under a now-sore lip but didn't feel any blood. Beth persuaded the pliable branches to relax toward the window. As she reached up to wind the wire along the longest branch, out past the tips of the leaves, a gust of wind frosted underneath the back of her sweater, making her shudder. Her teeth chattered. She wanted the sun to come back out and warm the air but she needed it to stay hidden for another five minutes until the plan was set in motion.

As Beth released the branch, the breeze forced it to tap the window. The metal extension she'd attached amplified the noise. Beth ran. At the back of the building by the rear entrance, she careened around the corner not even bothering to look. She and Jeremy both had classes in this building and knew the layout by heart.

Beth crashed into the mostly empty garbage drum and sent it spinning on its side toward the doors. Then, she cantered around the opposite side, rubbing her knee but keeping as low a profile as possible. Voices and shouts came from inside neared the back and far side of the building. Beth rounded the front and watched as the cop stationed at the double-door looked over his shoulder and then disappeared from sight. She trilled a robin's call. Jeremy came scrambling around the base of the stairs at the far side the same time she did.

Beth's heart pounded her chest, demanding to be released as she grabbed Jeremy's hand and leapt up the six sweeping steps to the door, in clear view of anyone who might be standing there. Beth yanked the door open, shoved Jeremy through the crack, slipped in, and twirled him around to the side stairwell. He stumbled going down, but they couldn't afford to stop.

At the bottom of the vestibule she dragged him into the closest classroom and landed in his lap on the floor. His hot breath warmed her ear and the side of her neck. She held onto him, quaking, waiting to hear the stampede of police swarming down the stairs after them.

There was no telling if they'd already swept this floor or not, so they couldn't afford the luxury of remaining locked in each other's arms for long. And Beth certainly didn't want to look closer at how her body reacted to Jeremy's touch.

They untangled their limbs and stood up. She kept her thoughts neutral and her steps steady. Grabbing Jeremy's hand, Beth gave it a squeeze and they were off again – down a connecting hall between the two sides of the building and, over to the far wall. The black door with the layers of mottled paint, rejecting the smooth metallic surface, beckoned her.

*The Boiler Room – where you didn't go if you were afraid of getting burned.*

They went in. Beth's breath echoed in the steel and galvanized chamber. Jeremy walked behind her as she maneuvered around the custodian's desk and the round table run by the Business Entrepreneurial students every second Sunday of the month, for midnight Poker buy-ins. They had other folding card tables hidden in nooks and crannies throughout this space, and students were known to access it from either the William Small or Strong basement. Beth had been invited by Jamie and the gang after a late rehearsal one night. They each received five chips for helping set up. Beth hadn't lasted long and left shortly after. She had too many tells.

The assorted vent tubes, A/C units, furnaces, and general pipes and wall ladders contributed to the maze-like quality of this nearly two-storey utility room. It spanned the length of two large classes, under the commons. Sweat made holding hands kinda gross, so Beth helped Jeremy find a belt loop on the back of her jeans to hold instead. He slipped a finger through the loose, worn loop, but chose to grip her hip instead of making a fist. The heat of his hand radiated through her pants and onto her skin. Just as she thought her heart had finally settled from "not getting caught", it bounded around in her chest like Tigger on steroids.

"There's an alcove about ten paces back, just past the transformer box. We can hide there."

Beth nodded and sighed. "Okay." Even as she led him around, some part of her refused to acknowledge the fact he couldn't see. Everything he did screamed independence and normalcy. Even the way he held her belt loop felt intimate and not necessitated. Guys didn't just casually hold onto her. Heck, her last relationship had been in high school. But after prom and different schools they'd simply fallen out of touch. Not even a messy goodbye to cling to as an excuse to avoid men.

She turned sideways and shimmied past a particularly bulbous section of round ductwork beside the transformer, then practically fell into an alcove of poured-concrete, squared but U-shaped, pulling Jeremy behind her. As she braced her hands against the wall to stop herself from falling, his one free arm came up beside her head. His hand connected with the wall above; Jeremy's shoulder and the side of his body followed.

As he shifted to help regain his bearings, the length of his body pressed against hers. His warm breath flowed down the nape of her neck. He slid his hand from her hip, but the motion turned her away from the wall and toward him. Her shoulder scraped the opposite wall of the small space.

"Shhh," he whispered in her ear, stilling her against him with both arms holding her – not nearly as tightly as she wanted. Beth tried to breathe through the ache in her chest and the pull of her sensibilities, or lack thereof.

No footsteps.

No noise except for the soft hum of the furnace kicking on.

She could only hope they'd swept the basement already or the cops had checked this portion of the Boiler Room when they'd searched the other building.

Beth shifted to face him, felt his body respond to their nearness. *Does he feel the same way? Or is that just an involuntary reaction?* She pressed her back against the wall to give him space to pull himself together, but he cocked his head to one side and gave her that sly grin. She couldn't help but foolishly grin back. *Maybe...*

She lifted his hand from her waist and placed his fingers against her lips so he could feel her reaction. They danced, ever so lightly across her mouth, and then over her ear, smoothing a stray strand of hair. Every nerve in her body sizzled. Still, the truth pelted ice-rain on her flesh. He leaned in, their noses hovering, separated only by the current arcing between them. She closed her eyes.

"I'm not your type," Beth's lips betrayed.

She heard him grin. "Says who?"

"Me. I've seen you. What turns your head, makes you pick up your feet. You're like a bloodhound."

He chuckled. "Perhaps. They are a type. I'll agree with you there. The type who likes to have fun and then move on. No strings attached."

"Exactly."

Jeremy pulled Beth closer until only clothes separated flesh from flesh. Every curve hugged every curve as his hands wrapped around her waist then down to the small of her back. Their lips brushed together. Her body shuddered, wanting to give over, to turn off her mind and just fall into the moment.

The nearness of him, taut arm muscle, the solid feel of his chest pressing against hers couldn't be real. The plain girl only got the hot guy *after* she'd been transformed. Beth was still Beth.

His lips hovered over her ear, taunting. "And why do you think that is? Why would I purposefully keep a woman at arm's length?"

She almost said, *because you're a player,* but that was her first impression, not the truth. Beth was afraid to think of the hurt little boy with the dog; the boy who'd been forced to build walls and learn to live blind… the child who grew into a man. He'd let her in. Not anyone else. Just as she'd let him get past her firewall of sensibility.

In answer, she slid her hands up over his tight abs and broad chest, drawing them together in a fevered kiss. Beth slipped her arms around his neck, climbing his lean form, falling into the heat of their bodies in that tight alcove.

Jeremy hadn't noticed her that first meeting, not really. Beth knew that. Zoned out, nothing registered until the end of the evening, once the group's TA planning was done. Sure, he'd smelled that girl's perfume, but if Beth was honest, she knew nothing phased him until the work was done. That alone said something. Jeremy had shown Moxie the formulas, been a team player.

And that second meeting, when he could have simply brushed her off and gone after the girl he'd been following out of the pub – he hadn't. He also hadn't simply switched from one target to the next, *her*. Jeremy knew she was different. Somehow, he knew she was lonely, too.

Sex, in the middle of a clandestine operation to find a bomb, might make sense in the movies, but Beth knew Jeremy was just as aware of their time constraints. He never slipped a hand up her shirt or tried to unbutton her jeans, but his lips found those tender places behind her ears and along the nape of her neck... the hollow of her throat. And their bodies learned every contour of each other regardless the layers of cloth separating them.

Jeremy broke off a deep, lingering kiss with a groan and set Beth back on the floor. Holding her, his back arched as he pressed his head against the concrete wall behind, reining himself in. She put a buffer of hot air between them, but only just. Their breathing slowed then he turned her toward the opening, slipped his finger through her belt loop, and gripped Beth's hip once more. She gave a shaky, nerve-laden laugh, trying to force the last of the pent-up energy from her body.

He was right, of course. They'd have time to discover each other later. Once Jeremy's cutting-edge fuel warmed up enough to release its scent, it would game over. It was the only thing that made sense. Wayne wanted to torture Jeremy as long as possible without being found. So, even though the fuel could be ignited while cold, Wayne was likely just using the smell as part of his timer somehow, like Jeremy said. These guys were chemistry majors, after all, and even though Jeremy was clearly miles ahead of Wayne, that guy was just devious enough to pin everything on his rival.

Beth slid past the last narrow opening and stumbled into the open office space that mirrored the opposite side. *We're in.* As far as she knew, nothing untoward happened on this side of the Boiler Room. Students just used it for a more covert way to arrive or leave the poker games. Beth shifted Jeremy's grip from her hip to her hand.

"Here's the other door."

They both pressed an ear to the metal barrier, straining to hear anything from the other side. Beth cracked the door open and they listened again.

Silence.

"Okay. Come on." She led him out into the basement hall of the Strong building and down the corridor. Mindful there could still be a police scout doing a final sweep as the main team worked on the William Small Centre, Beth hugged the walls and glanced around all corners as she led the way to the stairwell.

It was hard not to cause an echo as they climbed the steps to the ground floor, especially with the two of them moving through the space simultaneously. A tension headache jolted from the back of Beth's neck to the top of her skull. Holding her head, she ground her teeth and pushed through the pain. *Not now.* But stress had a way of frying her brain like nothing else.

Beyond the stairwell, a strange sensation of palpable weight in the air dulled her senses. Either that or the mix of adrenaline and impending migraine altered her awareness. The pressure of never knowing who might be around the next bend tightened invisible coils at the base of her neck. But she did her best to breathe through it and imagine each breath as wrapping around to cushion and dull the pain. That would only work for so long though.

Just down the corridor from the cafeteria, Beth led Jeremy into the common space. It had no doors, just two archways with a span of wall between. As they walked in, she looked up to the second-floor railing to make sure no one spied down on them from above. Jeremy let go of her hand and put his arms out as if getting a feel for the space. But when he turned a full-circle in the middle of the long room, his expression said so much more.

"What happened here, Jeremy?"

He shook his head. "Just look for the bomb."

"I told you, there's nowhere to hide a bomb in here. It's walls, floor, ceiling, and balcony."

"What's on the walls." It wasn't a question. The tone of his voice startled her. Beth let her gaze move this way and that instead of her head.

"Art."

"And over there?" He pointed to the box suspended chest-height on the wall and painted to look like it was open even though it wasn't. Some kind of comment on perception and shadows. Her class had used it to hold a variety of props during their performance. Now, the last thing she wanted to do was go near it. Her breath hitched. A spike of pain made it all the way to her right eye. She cradled her head in one hand.

"Are you okay?" He was suddenly only inches away, close enough to touch but not – a chasm opened between them. Being in this room had done something to him, and it wasn't just the bomb.

"Migraine coming."

Jeremy let his gaze track her voice. Beth swore he stared right at her, his crazy-pale husky-dog eyes piercing right through her. Through her and to the art box on the wall behind. Beth stutter-stepped back then turned her head, the last part of her body to follow.

She stared at the innocuous piece of art and slowly reached out to touch it. *Why here? What went down? How on earth does this relate back to Wayne?* Sparks of white flashed in front of Beth's eyes. She squeezed her lids tight then blinked rapidly before refocusing on the box attached to the wall, only slightly bigger than her head.

The stiffness in her arms made reaching out painful. She shook them at her side then tried again. Only her shoulders carried the extra tension now. Tracing her fingertips over the box, she searched for a way to open it. The edges of the wood felt rough. Not enough to cause a splinter, but not smooth like the surface either. The paint filled in most of the imperfections but she was able to follow a bead of dried glue all the way around the exhibit.

She breathed out. "It's not here." Beth dropped her hands allowing her shoulder to fall against the painted concrete-block wall beside it. Leaning her head against the wall's coolness, she closed her eyes. Relief clashed with shock and dread. Her body trembled. *Three strikes, you're out.*

Jeremy's voice strained against his anger. "That's impossible. Check again."

"No." Leaning her back against the wall, Beth slid down until she sat on the laminate-tile floor covering yet another layer of concrete, and let the cold seep into her bones. She felt him walk over and heard the rasp of skin on wood as he shifted around the damn box looking for something that wasn't there, again.

He hit the box. The crack made Beth jolt, sending a bolt of lightning through her skull and threatening to explode her eyeball.

"What the fuck, Jeremy!" Yelling only made it worse, but she couldn't help herself. "Why? Why are we doing this? The cops will underst−"

"How do you know!" he raged, turning to the room. His voice echoed throughout both floors. If someone was here, they'd find them now. "It's got to be here. This is the only place that truly makes sense. This is where he got his revenge."

Beth held her head with both hands, elbows resting on her knees, eyes still closed. "What are you talking about?"

"The Batman joke. He's laughing at me because he's exacting the ultimate revenge − finishing what he started last year."

"I don't understand." Beth cracked one eye and watched Jeremy pace a perfect rectangle in the middle of the room.

"Moxie wanted to start a kickboxing club, and when he got the 'okay' from the powers-that-be we set up a sparring session on mats in this room. Anyone who'd been part of a club previously was encouraged to attend and show off their stuff. Ground rules were set and posted, and for the next two hours we had an avid audience with lots of participants. Then, just after Moxie and I agreed to one last spar, Wayne's voice carries over the crowd claiming the final challenge – with me."

Beth had a feeling she knew where this was going, what she hadn't anticipated was a full demonstration. Jeremy re-enacted his side of the story within the rectangular grid he'd paced out moments before.

"It was fairly standard stuff at first. Nothing I couldn't handle. I heard him shift right and followed his breath sounds around the space. I was tired after alternating sessions with Moxie and let my guard down, assuming Wayne would continue to take it easy."

Jeremy shifted to the balls of his feet, moved back, did a half-turn fake-out, ducked down, kicked out with his right foot, then froze.

"He'd turned inside my kick and stomped on my left foot. It happened so fast." He lowered his leg and stood facing the floor as if watching the memory of himself crumble to the ground. "The turn was legit. The cleverly disguised stomp was not. Against the rules and no one saw. I had been unbeaten in every pairing – the blind guy. A smattering of applause, some hoots and hollers from the balcony, but mostly laughter. No one realized he'd fractured my baby toe. They just congratulated him on the win and then Moxie's crew took apart the mats. Moxie helped me over to a chair then went off to talk to a group of girls interested in joining the club."

"Why didn't you say something?" Beth whispered, more to keep the lightning in her head quiet than anything else. This whole situation with Wayne burned like acid in the pit of her stomach. She wanted to throw up, scream, melt into oblivion…

"I tried. They thought I was faking it. Saving face."

Beth rested her head against the wall and slowly rocked it back and forth. The new pressure-point temporarily diverted the bolt from her eyeball. She didn't want to move. They were still no closer to finding the bomb. No closer to stopping the insanity.

"Wayne doesn't care."

"What's that?"

"Wayne doesn't care about how you made him feel, and this was not as big a win in his books as you'd like to think. People were laughing, sure. But you weren't humiliated. He wants to bring you down so low, make you feel like the gum scraped off the bottom of someone's shoe, because that's how he feels whenever he's compared to you."

A buzzing started somewhere deep in her brain and the reflux instinct came back so fast the nausea made her flatten her arms against the wall for stability as she gulped air. But her blood roiled. He was being pig-headed and stubborn, and she just wanted to feel safe again.

"Have you ever been terrified, Jeremy? I mean, other than when you lost your sight. Here, on campus? Have you ever been so bone-numbingly freaked out that you almost gave up? Because *that* is where he will have hidden the bomb. Not where you made him feel like shit. Not where you made a mockery of him. He's just giving that right back to you. Building your fear as time ticks past to the point of no return. He doesn't want you to save the day. He wants you petrified to the point of inaction so that this is your fault."

She pushed herself up the wall, walking her hands behind her while trying to keep her head still. Forcing her eyes open, Beth squinted past the shards of light attacking her retina to the still figure silhouetted in the middle of the room. She'd made a promise, but it was one she couldn't keep. It was time to end this. It was time to be not just the voice of reason, but the action.

"Come on. We're leaving," she said.

He didn't move.

"Jeremy, it's time to tell the cops."

"I can't. I have to stop him. Stop this. You're right, it *is* my fault," he said.

"You can't do this alone. *Come on!*" Beth staggered toward the door. He'd follow if he thought she was really leaving. *He'll follow.*

She stumbled down the hall, first holding her head, then her stomach. Her body understood. She couldn't do this. Couldn't chase after a bomb that might explode any minute. Couldn't sacrifice herself for love… she just wasn't strong enough.

Beth crashed through the front door, tripping over her own feet and falling, falling, falling… into a pair of strong, solid arms. Her heart leapt as she cracked open her eyes, but it wasn't Jeremy who looked back.

# HISTORY LESSON

I t wasn't until Jeremy heard Beth crash through the front door that he clued in. *She's gone.* She'd actually walked right out the building. The sudden commotion of abrupt yells and stern voices meant she wasn't coming back either. She'd really left him. Suddenly, the empty space around him grew, or maybe he shrank now that she was gone. Beth had promised to help, had done so much... maybe he'd asked too much.

Breaking through his daze, Jeremy blended into the walls and slunk off in the opposite direction. His mind continued to attack her logic even as he focused on a new objective – *find the back door*. Luckily, he knew this building well and headed for the cafeteria. Strong College had the best burgers on campus.

Beth's warning echoed in his mind, *He doesn't want you to find the bomb. He wants you terrified. He wants you out of the way.* She hadn't said those exact words, but it was Beth's voice repeating them over and over in his mind.

Jeremy should have seen it sooner. Wayne didn't want

to hurt the university or the other people in it. This was all about discrediting Jeremy and removing the competition. He had no doubt in his mind a bomb actually existed, but Wayne would have put it in the one spot Jeremy would never think to go alone – to ensure his plan worked.

Jeremy slipped into the cafeteria and followed the wall around to the server entrance. A girl he'd met second year often took the closing shift and he'd offered to "help out" a few times. But he couldn't even muster a smile with the memory as he bypassed the heavy scent of greasy grill and burn-off to the windowless door set into the wall at the back.

Once outside, Beth's voice in his mind caused Jeremy to miscalculate his steps. He walked straight into a wall of bushes. Her voice brought swirls of blue and lavender and white, like clouds at dusk in a bruised sky. As a kid, he'd loved staring at the sky, lying on his back in the yard waiting for his dad to come home, even though he never did.

Jeremy swiped at a scratch on his cheek and felt a line of blood. He wiped it on his jeans, course corrected, and disappeared into the shrubbery via the worn dirt path, avoiding the main walkways. Time worked against him, a fact he couldn't ignore even as he leaned his shoulder against a familiar tree to regain his bearings.

The edge of anger in Beth's words, even when she'd whispered, had also betrayed her fear. He never should have asked her to risk her life for his stupid pride. Something hadn't been right since they kissed in the Boiler Room. She wasn't normally that forward, that eager. He'd loved the taste of her – salty-sweet – but never realized the tension and tight coil of nerves inherent in doing something dangerous might also push her beyond her usual bubble of comfort. But would she have gone there, done that, if she didn't already feel that way about him? Maybe that scared her too…

His forehead smacked the flat of a no littering sign. It wasn't the first time either. He should have realized it was an omen, but being sloshed after a three-day bender during Frosh Week, all those years ago, prevented him from thinking clearly. Just as Beth did today. Jeremy rubbed his head, side-stepped, then took a deep breath and forced himself to concentrate.

The SRU were still sweeping the east quadrant. As soon as they were done with the buildings, they'd be heading this way to cover all bases. Jeremy had to get to the bomb first. He had no idea how he'd dismantle it once he got there, but he'd figure that out later. Maybe it was a hoax. Maybe Wayne… but Jeremy just wasn't that lucky.

At the edge of a walking path that skirted the forest closest to the campus-proper, Jeremy crouched low in the bushes and concentrated on his surroundings. The squawk of a blue jay overpowered the gentler tones of bonded mourning doves. Neither species seemed particularly unsettled by their environment – a good sign. Construction crews worked on nearby roads to beat the first lasting blast of snow, and vehicles drove past the far boundary for the campus. No traffic whatsoever on the school roads or closest main road.

*It's about time I got a break.* Jeremy shot free of the bushes and crossed the interlocking stone path, eight full strides, to the deer path twining through more densely packed trees. A blast of wind made him curl in on himself as it pierced his sweater. The sharp scent of pine needles and the crackle of underbrush told him he'd breached the forest's perimeter. Forcing his arms wide, he felt the tree needles, bare branches, and dried thistles edging the path. All he had to do was follow it, winding as it did, through the forest to the open field. Sweeping one foot in front of the other, he moved as fast as he dared.

Eight other Chem-frosh had staggered through the trees with him that night, seven years ago. The sun had cooled but he'd still felt it on his bare skin. They were all shirtless, torsos painted with varying compounds for alcohol – even the girls; but they got to keep their bras on, or so he'd heard. They were on a scavenger hunt with one last item to find. Only two of them would be crowned the Chem Masters. The clue, which they'd all received verbally, led them to the forest and ultimately the field in its midst.

He remembered bumping into the corner of a table, set out in the middle of the clearing, and sloshing yet more alcohol over a set of steins. They had to chug the contents and return with their stein to win. But it hadn't been just any alcohol… it was chem-lab moonshine. The ginger ale diluting it was meant to be a joke. Well, they'd all chugged and the last thing Jeremy remembered was taking two steps back the way they'd come and blacking out. He'd woken, chilled and alone, with zero sense for bearings, and a raging hangover. The next morning, Campus Patrol found him curled up under the table shivering uncontrollably.

They'd all known he was blind. But they also knew they had to get back before everyone else to be "crowned", and being wasted meant no one remembered where they'd last seen him.

A sharp branch poked him in the forehead above his left eye. He'd gotten lax and forgotten to check above him as well as beside. Stepping into a rut, he rolled his ankle and fell into a thorny bush. As he yanked back against their grabbing canes his now exposed forearm slammed into a broken limb, gouging his flesh. Stumbling backward, he tripped over a dead branch, fell, and cracked his head against the hard-packed earth. Jeremy's heart thundered as it beat to escape his chest as even the light and grey shadows before his eyes went black.

He blinked. *I'm not unconscious.* He reached for his face to touch his eyes. Blood dripped from the slice on his arm onto his face. He jolted, then wiped his cheek and nose with the other arm of his sweater. *Why's everything dark? What happened? What's going on?*

The Mario Bros. theme song played a second time. Jeremy shivered and his random arm swipes, laced with needle-sharp pain, launched him into frantic searching. *Not again. Not again.* Between struggling to process insulin, no food in over twelve hours, and the increased stress, his body had given up on him. He groaned. *How long have I been out?* He listened for sounds of commotion from the direction of the bomb. Nothing. Constant black suffocated his perception of light and dark. *Get your fat ass up,* his high school coach growled in his head. The Mario tune played again. He rolled over and yanked the phone from his back pocket.

"Hello?" he rasped. "Elle?"

Muffled voices, sounding far more official than anyone he knew, came over the line. It was the cops *and Elle!* He listened as she explained everything to the cops, but they still didn't believe her. Until…

"Oh my God," she said. "I know where the bomb is."

*Shit.* Jeremy scrambled to roll over and get up. He staggered, falling back to his knees, woozy. Reaching for his head, he brushed his arm and felt blood. A lot of blood. He fumbled the phone and the line went dead, but it didn't matter.

They were coming.

They were coming, and he had to get to the bomb first.

## SUPER GIRL, WONDER WOMAN, AND BETH

Beth felt a little floaty. Whatever the medic gave her for the migraine was potent stuff. She blinked and tried to focus on the SRU officer not three feet in front of her.

"You said you had information on the bomber. What can you tell me?"

She had demanded to speak with the person in charge as soon as the explosions in her brain dulled to distant storms. "It's not Jeremy Palmer. He's involved but he didn't make the bomb." Beth heard herself with an echo and tried to shake it from her head. She'd left him.

*What was I thinking?*

*You'd thought he'd follow you.*

*He thought I was bluffing.*

*He's going after that thing alone, you know.*

"Yes, we're aware of that. What makes you think he didn't do it?"

She didn't like the sound of that. Jeremy was right.

They were convinced it was him. *Dammit. I have to warn him. But I'm here and he's there and...* her brain wasn't working right. *If he dies...* she couldn't finish the thought. Beth grabbed her phone from the back pocket of her jeans and slid it into the pouch on the front of her sweater. She shivered and tucked both hands inside doing her best to find the right speed-dial.

"I've been with Jeremy searching for the damn thing for the past two hours." She took in a shaky breath as the medic wrapped a thin, silver, emergency blanket around her shoulders. Beth breathed out slow, trying to find order to her thoughts, to calm down. And that's when the truth stabbed at her, digging deep and twisting the blade of regret.

"I know him. He loves this place. He's trying to earn a position working on his Masters after he graduates this year – and he's succeeding. Did he make the bomb? No. Is he responsible for the fuel used in the bomb? Yes. It was supposed to be a theoretical assignment to base his Masters thesis from and he wanted to make sure it was viable. That it wasn't just a bunch of numbers saying the right thing on the screen. *Wayne* is behind this. Not Jeremy." *Oh God, what have I done?*

"And you say this Wayne person feels slighted by Jeremy's success and stole his experiment, weaponized it no less, just to get back at him? You expect me to believe–"

"Wayne wants Jeremy out of the way. There's only one position available with that prof. They're in competition and Jeremy's winning. I doubt Wayne would target a heavily populated area, he still wants to go to school here, he's just trying to isolate..."

"Isolate what?" the officer asked, confused.

A brief moment of clarity came across Beth. Her yelling at Jeremy about being vulnerable. About Wayne putting the bomb the last place Jeremy would go. The night Jeremy apologized and explained about being blind, *what had he said? Something about sticking to his mental paths because of a bad experience during frosh week...* and then it hit her–

"Oh my God. I know where the bomb is!"

The Captain shifted forward. "Where? Where is it?"

"The only place on campus Jeremy ever felt scared. The field in the middle of the forest on the far side of the school." He stuck to familiar places on purpose, because of what happened frosh week. He'd asked her to be his eyes so he wouldn't have to do this alone. She'd promised him... and then broke that promise. Beth had to make this right.

"I have two sweeper teams going through the buildings on that side of campus as we speak. Are you sure? If I redirect one and the bomb is somewhere else–"

"Then take another team. I can show you. Take you right to the place. We don't have time–"

The officer stood up from the bumper of the ambulance, shifting the weight off the back end. He radioed for back up and several officers came out of the two black vans and from inside the stadium within seconds of his call. Beth stood up to walk over to their circle but he gave her a warning look to stay back before briefing the team. *Not good.*

"The girl is certain she knows where the bomb is. We'll

take a third team into the east quadrant based on her directions–"

"No. You have to take me with you." She stepped up to the circle of imposing officers. The man in charge waved off the female cop moving to intercept Beth and instead, he turned into Beth's bubble of comfort, slowly walking her backward until her knees bumped the ambulance. She forced herself to remain standing.

"I know you mean well, but there's no way we're taking a civilian to a suspected bomb location. We don't have time to–"

"No, you don't have time. That bomb could go off at any moment and the longer it takes you to get there, the more likely Jeremy will get hurt. If I figured this out, then so has he. We had the same conversations and he's been lucid longer than me. He's *blind*. Don't you get that? He's going to attempt to disarm a bomb by himself. Let me show you exactly where this thing is."

Beth glared at him and he stared through her.

"Sarge, you can't seriously be considering taking her with us?" A hovering officer from the circle asked.

The Sergeant looked at Beth. "Can we drive there?" he asked.

Some of the tightness lifted from her chest. "Most of the way. The forest thins closer to the main road."

"Okay. Let's go."

Beth never felt a hand placed on her, and yet they managed to usher her into the van just from their proximity and positioning. She sat shotgun and directed the wheel-man on the fastest route to the east forest. Jeremy's frosh group hadn't been the only one to use the location as part of an unofficial orientation. But, other than the theatre students, no one used it during the year and it was getting on the cold side now, so Wayne wouldn't even be placing those students at risk. Just Jeremy.

A floor to ceiling door-cage separated the back operations portion of the van from her and the driver. The team worked on any number of logistical things, their words washing over her as she concentrated on the road. Within two minutes, the van jumped the curb and four-wheeled it over the manicured grass toward the edge of the forest.

The second the van stopped, Beth jumped out of the vehicle along with a fully-strapped team plus bomb gear. She froze for a split second. *What if I'm wrong? What if the bomb isn't here? What if Wayne never made a bomb, just stole Jeremy's stuff to make him think he did?* Panic gripped her chest making it hard to breathe.

"All right, where to Beth?" The Sergeant's intense gaze shattered the ice in her veins. She turned and ran – straight for the dirt path beyond the treeline. Even though the SRU carried fifty or more pounds each of heavy gear, they easily kept pace and followed her fast-weave through the trees. Her heartbeat double-timed to her footfalls. She knew Jeremy would never give up, and if Wayne did weaponize the fuel, Jeremy would risk his life to neutralize it. That wasn't something Beth was prepared for.

Her high school friends had all moved or attended school hours away. Trying to make new friends, people who "got her" and wanted to spend time with her as much as she did with them... well, that was a pipe-dream until two weeks ago. A flash of heat surged through her at the memory of their bodies glued to each other in the Boiler Room… that kiss… Even if she didn't already owe it to Jeremy because she'd broken her promise, she owed it to herself and the glimpse of what could be to make sure he didn't get blown up today.

Beth burst through the edge of the forest and ran a dozen steps into the dry, low, grassy field and stopped. There, in the middle of nowhere, maybe another ten yards in, sat a small camo-tent made from netting. It was the kind of thing her Great Uncle Morris might use to keep mosquitos off the BBQ platter at the cottage. She stepped back and walked into the wall that was the Sergeant.

"We need to fall back. We'll send in the RBDU."

"The what?" Beth turned and hurried back to the edge of the treeline with him.

"Robot Bomb Detection Unit."

"Oh. Of course."

The team nearly had it assembled. There were two units: one that rode on treads, and one drone. She glanced back over her shoulder and her heart dropped. A figure shifted away from the shadow of the trees on the opposite side of the field.

"Jeremy." She turned back around and ran. "Jeremy, No!" She vaguely registered a hand nearly grabbing the hood of her sweatshirt, but the adrenaline shrieking through her veins propelled her with superhuman speed toward the only guy who'd ever bothered to get to know her. Who'd actually heard her sing, listened to her terrible puns, gave her that cocky, mischievous smile, and made her insides go supernova with just a touch.

But the dark, lanky, Ashton Kutcher-like silhouette made her stumble over her own feet, not two yards from that little food tent.

It wasn't Jeremy.

It was Wayne.

## NOT A DC COMIC

"Dammit!" Jeremy punched a half-fallen rotted tree trunk. Feeling the soggy wood beneath his knuckles split and crumble helped bleed the frustration from his body. But now his hand hurt after hitting a rock beneath the log. He'd staggered around the forest in circles, trying to find the path again. The fall and blacking out, along with everything else that was wrong with him, made him lose his bearings.

He heard a large engine bounce its vehicle over a curb off to his right. *Must be from the main road.* Since he woke, only the squawk of birds and crunch of dried leaves sounded. *They're here.* A black weight, as dark as his sight and as heavy as a truck, sat on his chest. *At least they'll get to the bomb before it blows.* He had no idea what he was going to do once he'd found it. He knew he'd figure it out. Rotating his body toward the commotion on the other side of the forest, Jeremy limped toward the inevitable.

It was his fault, really. He never should have taken the new fuel out of theoretical calculations. Professor Young would have been impressed, even with one of the less defined early versions. Still, Jeremy had to make sure Wayne didn't propose something even better, more plausible. School was his life, and becoming a legit TA researching under the foremost leading scientist at the university meant he might never have to leave. First a Masters, then a PhD, and then... maybe even a full-time teaching position. But now, now he'd go to jail and face–

"Jeremy, No!" Elle screamed, terror shredding her voice.

Fear streaked through Jeremy's heart. Pushing his hands up he leapt into a sprint, crashing through the treeline toward her voice and staggering onto the field. But a silence, so absolute even the birds and the wind stopped, made his guts drop.

The blast echoed as a wave of energy forced him to his knees. An agonizing shriek laced with surprise tore at his hollowed-out insides. Heat radiated from the explosion. Jeremy scrambled forward, pushing past the pain in his ankle, in his arm, his hand.

"Check her vitals!" a gruff voice shouted. "Get her away from the blast site ASAP." Other voices layered over the first as walkie-talkies clicked on and off. Another shuffling commotion by the trees, off to his left, assaulted his senses.

"Let go of me! He's the one you want!"

*Wayne?*

And then an arm clotheslined Jeremy just as the wail of an ambulance pierced the air. The officer rolled Jeremy over and slapped a pair of handcuffs on him.

"You have the right to remain silent. You have the right to an attorney."

"What? No. No, I have to get to Elle. Beth. Elspeth. Fuck!" Jeremy squirmed against his binds and the man gripping his arms. "Please. You don't understand. Is she all right? Where is she? I heard her scream."

"We've got a pulse. Let's get her on the stretcher. Ready? One. Two. Three."

Jeremy heard a thump but no groan or yell, or anything from Elle.

"You don't understand. I'm Jeremy. She said she was going to tell you about me. About everything. Please, I didn't do this. Wayne Fischer did."

"He's lying! I've been following him. Trying to figure out why he's leading an innocent girl away from the evacuation toward a bomb."

"Shut up," the cop holding him growled.

"Pleeeease!" Jeremy turned to the officer. "I would never hurt her. I love her. She was helping me look for the bomb *he* made using my chem experiment. I didn't want to risk getting thrown out of school. We were supposed to find it, disarm it, and make sure no one got hurt."

He heard the stretcher wheel past him and through the trees.

"Let me go with her. I have to. You don't understand. I'm not the bad guy. I'm not the bomber. I've been trying to stop this from happening."

But they just kept walking, the officer steering him this way and that through the trees. Jeremy heard the stretcher wheels collapse as they connected with the rear of the ambulance as the unit slid into place. Beth still hadn't said anything.

He didn't know what else to say, what else to do. As the door to a van slid open, Jeremy turned one last time, pushing his hands and back against the side of the vehicle. In a split-second he calculated the approximate height of the cop based on the position of his arm, and the general physical aura of the man.

Jeremy's eyes wavered in their dark, shadow-less shroud, searching for a face he'd never see – settling on the most likely place he could calculate, hoping to lock gazes. But he couldn't keep the waver from his chin or the tears from splashing from his un-seeing eyes.

"Please," he whispered one last time. His head grew light again and he slumped against the vehicle.

The lengthening silence tore at his sanity.

"Hold up!" the officer called over his shoulder. "Jimmy, ride up front. Jeremy needs medical attention, too. I'm putting him in the back with the girl."

"Sure thing, Sarge." The front door to the ambulance opened and shut. The Sergeant pulled Jeremy forward and unlocked his cuffs before steering him over to the back of the emergency vehicle.

"He's got minor lacerations all over but a deep gouge on his arm. The sleeve is covered in blood. He's light-headed, might have lost a lot of blood. Check his ankle, too, he's been limping. The girl also mentioned he's a Type-Two diabetic who's been off his meds for nearly a week."

Jeremy pulled his meds from his pocket. A hand from inside the ambulance grabbed his arm to help him up. The long, slender fingers ended by digging moon shapes into his flesh a little. A woman.

"Sit here," she said as the doors slammed shut. He dropped to a low stool near the cab of the vehicle and listened as the two EMTs, one male, one female, worked together. A cabinet snapped open and a bag of liquid sloshed as the man lifted it up and slid it into place. The drip. The woman kept talking low to her until the guy shifted in front of Jeremy, blocking him from Elle. The bump back over the curb was minimal as the driver took them to the hospital.

"What happened to your arm?" the female EMT asked.

He explained about the woods, the trouble with his medication, the fall… but he couldn't muster any effort to his words.

"Is she your girlfriend?"

"Yeah."

"Here, shift forward a bit and give me your good arm." The sirens bleeped and wailed. They were probably passing through an intersection with traffic, beyond the empty roads cordoned-off around campus.

She lifted his hand and placed it over Elle's. He curled his fingers around hers but she didn't move. He tried to stifle a sob.

"Hey, now. She's stable but the blast knocked her out. All we can do is keep her comfortable, make sure her vitals don't change, and wait for her to wake up. Now, I need you to hold still."

Jeremy nodded.

The EMT cut open the sleeve of his sweater in one quick slice.

"Will she, you know, wake up? Or are you just saying that?" He cringed from the antiseptic she basted over his arm and gritted his teeth.

"Why don't you talk to her? Let her know you're here?"

He leaned forward and knocked his head against the corner of a bulkhead or storage cabinet but left if there and closed his already dark eyes. Tears pushed past his lids and drew lines on his cheeks down to his chin. He couldn't talk to her. Not here.

Weren't the good guys supposed to save the day? Not get blown up and arrested? He managed a shaky breath and tried to hold it, and the tears, in. But the burning fire in his chest was from more than lack of air. He hadn't let himself dare to think it before, but he knew she was the one.

"Oh, Elspeth…" he whispered.

And then, half a breath later, she gave his fingers the tiniest squeeze.

## NORMALITY IN THE MIDST OF CHAOS

Jeremy sat on a waiting room chair with his head down, slumped forward with his elbows on his knees. His bandaged arm throbbed, a constant reminder that this was his fault. A uniformed officer stood nearby – Jimmy. He'd heard doctors and nurses walk through these halls with quickened steps and hushed voices. The worst was hearing the frantic rise in Beth's mom's voice asking after her daughter before she and Beth's dad were escorted to a private waiting room. The EMT had told Jeremy that Elle was stable. She'd squeezed his hand, too. But at the hospital, no one spoke to him. He only knew she had to undergo a barrage of tests to make sure she hadn't suffered internal injuries.

"Jeremy Palmer?" a polite, female voice asked.

He raised his head toward the speaker but didn't even try to hide his blindness. Didn't even try to connect with her.

"Elspeth is asking for you."

He rose, unsteady. "She's okay? The tests?"

"Walk with me. She can tell you about the results when you see her." The woman's voice faltered at her choice of words. He didn't care. The raw ache that tore at his insides tensed with his entire body.

"May I take your elbow?" he asked.

"Of course. Here it is." She led him to her arm, and they left the waiting room. Another set of heavy footsteps followed. "She's been settled in room 3011. We'll be keeping her overnight and monitoring her for the next few days. Visiting hours are 9:00 a.m. to 8:00 p.m. You'll want to check with Elspeth about her scheduled doctor's visits, but usually those happen well-before visitors arrive."

He felt her reach forward then stand tall again. A ding signified the arrival of an elevator. Several people stepped out and brushed past him before the nurse led him into a rather large box, the officer following. His two-way radio squawked occasionally. The elevator on campus always felt as though the walls pressed in on him. This one felt like the sink area of a washroom, not too open but maneuverable.

"And you say she's all right?"

"She's doing well and continues to be stable. Like I said, I'll let her tell you the rest."

A stab of fear made him cough. "Are her parents still there?"

He could almost hear the sad smile in her words. "They're taking a much-needed dinner break right now." Jeremy's skin flashed from hot to cold and back again, his nerves unable to settle. He swallowed repeatedly. The doors opened.

"This way," the nurse said, turning him to the left. He counted his steps, trying to keep a clear enough mind to find his way back again… *if she wants me to come back, that is.* A heavy surety settled in his chest, dragging his already tired limbs. *This is it. She's going to tell me to shove off. God, Jeremy, you don't blow up the only girl you've ever loved. Of course she never wants to see me again.*

They stopped at fourteen paces and she knocked on a partially open door. Closed doors sounded different.

"Elspeth? Jeremy's here." The nurse tugged his arm to enter and she placed him at the foot of the bed, hands resting on the mobile TV tray. She gave his arm a light squeeze, then left, closing the door behind her. Jimmy stayed out in the hall.

"You look like shit," Beth said.

"What? Uh… yeah, probably. Are you all right?" He wanted to shift around the side of the bed and hold her hand, but if this was the end of it all, Jeremy knew he'd better stay put.

She sighed. "I thought it was you. For some reason I'd convinced myself that, even without me there to help you, you'd still try to disarm that thing. But it wasn't you. It was Wayne."

He nodded, remembering the guy being caught about the same time as Jeremy. He let his chin drop to his chest. "I'm so sorry, Beth. I never meant to put you in harm's way. I– I– I don't know what I was thinking would happen… not this." He shrugged. He'd asked her to be his eyes but never once did it cross his mind that they wouldn't make it in time.

"I know. Come here. To my right, your left. I'm having trouble reading your lips."

"Reading my– What?" Jeremy walked his hands and body around to her right side.

"And it's Elle, remember? Aren't I supposed to be 'the girl'?"

*My girl. My friend.* He searched for her hand, gingerly holding it around a tube and tape. "What do you mean read my lips? I thought you were okay."

"They say I was far enough away that my insides didn't get damaged by the blast, but the hearing in my left ear is wonky. Not static, but like trying to make out voices under water – muffled and garbled."

"Will it come back?" His pulse spiked. She *was* hurt.

"Only time will tell." Her voice sounded strong at the words she'd probably heard a dozen times or more now. Jeremy shifted his stance and felt a chair behind his legs. He pulled it forward and sat down, holding her one hand with both of his.

"What about the fireball? Are you–"

"A little singed but no worse for wear. I tried to curl into a ball and keep low when the blast went off. That was wishful thinking, but I did manage to keep low enough that when it flamed up, and not out, I wasn't burned." The drop at the end of her words told him she was tired.

"I should go. Let you sleep. I'll come back." But she squeezed his hand when he shifted to rise just as the door swung open.

"Hey, lovey, we decided to bring dinner back here…" Two sets of footsteps entered the room, one obviously

Elle's mother and the other was not the officer – who had a decidedly different presence.

*Oh shit.* Jeremy tried to swallow, but there was nothing there to moisten his throat. The reason why their daughter lay in this hospital bed, now sat there holding her hand. He took in short, shallow breaths, cringing internally for the verbal blast.

"Jeremy?" Mrs. Donaldson asked.

He pursed his lips and nodded toward her voice, his entire being primed for being hauled bodily out the room.

She shifted, her feet shuffling and clothes rustling as if looking around, and then a deep, fatherly voice said, "Where are your parents, son?"

"M– My parents? I–" Jeremy turned toward Elle, confused. She squeezed his hand. Then, as he turned back a warm, slightly rounded "mom-body" engulfed his shoulders in a hug. He stiffened, jolting slightly.

"Yes, sweetie, your parents. Aren't they here?"

"Uh, no. My step-dad likes to winter in Arizona. I don't think they even know what's happened." Jeremy couldn't control the tremor in his voice. He hadn't even thought about them. Not to warn them there was a scare on campus, not to tell them he'd been treated at the hospital.

"Do you need us to call them for you, son?" Mr. Donaldson asked. Elle's mom released him from the hug and held him at arm's length, careful to avoid his injury.

"Uh, no. No, that's okay. They should hear about it from me." His eyes inadvertently shifted toward where the door should be, where the officer likely still stood guard. The world remained black, but the doctor had said it was likely temporary due to the lack of insulin, food, and high stress. Not to mention getting concussed out in the woods – all just part of the same mess. He frowned, not knowing what more to say or what Elle had told them. *Why are they being so nice?*

Paper bags shifted on the TV tray. "Grace, why don't we give them a few minutes? We'll just be down the hall checking on your schedule, hon."

Mrs. Donaldson let go of Jeremy and joined her husband out in the hall, closing the door but not pulling it all the way shut. The bouncing click told him they were willing to give them some privacy, but only so much.

"I– I don't understand. Why are your parents being so nice? Didn't you tell them what happened? Your dad should've tossed me out on my ass the second he laid eyes on me."

She gave a soft chuckle and then coughed. Elle shifted her hand away from his and reached over to her left. The suction of a straw on ice told him she'd needed a drink of water. Jeremy felt so helpless. He should have gotten that for her. She deserved so much more than he could ever give.

When her hand returned to his, she said, "I told them you were framed and we never really expected Wayne to have made a bomb. I said we were looking for your experiment so you couldn't be accused of something you didn't do. They know that what happened was an accident. They know I left you alone and that I got scared you'd risk hurting yourself trying to clear your name. *And* they know I had second thoughts. I felt guilty for abandoning you. I told them I was in love in with you."

"You did what?"

She laughed again. "I know. Crazy huh?"

"No. That's the least crazy thing I've heard all day." Jeremy slid his fingers along Elle's arm, up to her shoulder, neck, and face. Then he leaned over and kissed her ever so gently on the lips.

# GRADUATION

SEVEN MONTHS LATER

The warm, early June breeze lifted the tassel draped to the right of Beth's cap. She raised her arms to let the air flow through the large sleeves of her grad gown as she stood exposed to the full-sun at the side of the giant tent. It wasn't that there were no trees in the central common, but the double football-field length of space was exactly that... wide open with the mature trees hugging the perimeter.

Shifting forward at a snail's pace around the side of the structure, Beth couldn't help but smile at the caw of two seagulls fighting over the remains of someone's lunch nearby. The sound was clear, clean, and distinct. Sure, they were loud birds to begin with, but this time last month their cries would have still been garbled.

Now, the chatter of her classmates was another story. They kept their voices low, even in their excitement, and Beth was lucky to hear half of their giggled whispers if her bad ear faced them. Still, her doctor had said nothing was permanent, yet. All the studies he'd advised her to read up on said pretty much the same thing: wherever your hearing is at after a year, is likely where it will stay.

"–my Nona, five cousins, and my old high school gang," Gabriella listed everyone who came to support her sitting in the audience.

"Donny, Trina– gang are watching, too." Beth's hearing cut out again, but that wasn't what put the sad smile on her face. She had her mom and dad, a perpetuating story since elementary school grad. Beth loved them to pieces, but sometimes she just wished one of those dozens of connections over the years had lasted.

The line shuffled forward enough that she could slip into the shade of the structure just before turning down the make-shift hall leading to the wing on the side of the stage. All the chatter around her stopped as the girls, and even a few of the guys, straightened their robes and triple-checked to make sure their tassels hung on the right side.

Beth scanned the back of the heads in the audience as camera lights and smartphone flashes lit the cavernous space under the giant tent, every time another student shook hands with the Chair and Dean up on stage. The movement of a program used as a fan caught her eye. *Mom!* And her Dad pointed to something inside his own program as Mom leaned her head toward his shoulder to see. A warm comfort spread through Beth's chest. They'd found the place okay. Then, a curly blond sat up straight from the seat beside her mom and cocked his head in that tell-tale way he had when listening to a hushed conversation.

*Jeremy.*

And then the soft partition blocked her view. Mini-fireworks exploded inside Beth's body making her tingle all over. Jeremy had promised he'd be there, but she hadn't wanted to get her hopes up. His ankle monitor ensured his "house arrest" and he wasn't permitted anywhere on campus except for pre-approved locations to finish out his year. The police and the university hadn't even let him attend his own graduation. But he'd said he had a plan… said he'd try to arrange to return home today and temporarily have the restrictions lifted.

*He kept his promise.*

Had she kept hers, last November, neither of them might be in this situation. Still, Beth's therapist kept reminding her the only one at fault was Wayne. Had he minded his own business, none of this would have happened. Beth was just glad the jury saw fit to place the blame squarely on Wayne's shoulders. Once that verdict came through, Jeremy's parents' lawyer was able to negotiate a deal for a lesser charge. They let him finish his program and serve community hours while under "house arrest" on campus. He'd gotten to finish his final year at the very least, even though he'd desperately wanted more.

Beth stumbled a little going up the risers leading to the stage. A tech guy, dressed in a suit but no tie, raised his hand near his hip warning her to wait. She nodded then looked forward as Gabriella shook hands with the Dean and the Chair, turned to a barrage of camera flashes with her signature smile, gave a wave to all her extended family and friends then shifted her tassel to the left before bouncing down the stairs on the opposite side.

"Elspeth Lenore Donaldson," the caller read out her name.

Beth jolted a little then stepped out onto the stage. A chorus of whoops and hollers followed her every step. Confused, she risked a glance out to the audience and there, just to the left of Jeremy and her parents were the Theatre crew: Jamie, Kim, Wiz, and Tank. Beth hadn't seen them in ages... not since that day really. She'd put all her time into her studies and spent every spare minute with Jeremy, which wasn't nearly as often as she would've liked. And yet they were here, cheering her on like no time had passed. Maybe Jeremy wasn't the only one she'd been wrong about.

Pulling her gaze away from the audience, Beth focused instead on the Dean and the Chair of the Sociology Department. She'd practised for this with Jeremy, him pretending to be the Dean – left hand accepts the diploma, right hand goes over top to shake. Hold. Give the camera flashes five seconds, nod, shake the Chair's hand, wait a moment, and go.

As she stepped past the Chair, Beth turned toward the crowd, raised her diploma, and waved. Then, she shifted her tassel to the left and exited the stage.

Everyone was being ushered out a back opening and then around the opposite side of the tent to sit at the rear of the audience to watch the rest of the processional and the speeches. But just as she left the back way, and turned to follow the outside of the structure, Beth's cell buzzed in her pocket. She was going to leave it in her dorm, but today was the last day to hear if her marks had been good enough.

Beth hauled up the hem of her black robe exposing a pair of tan Capris, and retrieved her phone. The call display showed a university exchange. She took a deep breath to calm her racing heart then answered.

"Hello?"

"May I speak with Elspeth Donaldson?"

"Speaking."

"My name is Taylor and I'm calling from the Department of Sociology on campus to let you know that you've been selected as a top candidate for a second interview for the intern position."

"Really? That's wonderful."

"Are you available to come in next Wednesday, for one-thirty in the afternoon?"

"Yes." Beth had until Friday to clear out of her dorm and nothing else booked for the week, just in case.

"Excellent. We'll see you then."

Beth didn't even have time to put her phone away. She looked up with a giant smile and got scooped up into Jamie's famous bear hug.

"Grrrr," he growled and twirled her around. "Congratulations, punk. You did it. Suma Cum Laude. That's awesome." When he put her down, Kim, Wiz, and Tank sandwiched her in another hug. Then, feeling left out, Jamie wrapped his arms around all four of them and they staggered around in a fit of giggles. Beth looked up as she and her friends untangled their bodies from the group hug. And there Jeremy stood, leaning casually with his arms crossed against the taut outer edge of the massive tent, a crazy grin stuck on his face.

Beth broke free of her friends and ran over to him,

slowing as he stepped away from the tent. For the first time in six months they were out of his room and away from the surveillance cameras. The gang slapped Beth on the back and shoulders telling her in a loud whisper they'd meet her in the Grad Lounge after the speeches, and then headed over that way. The classmate who was behind Beth in line, slipped around her and Jeremy as they stood there, inches apart, and yet still not touching.

Beth reached for his hand and pulled him from the path of Grad traffic over to a tree by the edge of the common. When they stopped, she snagged his other hand and they spoke near simultaneously.

"I have good news."

"I just got word," he said.

"You first." Her body ached to be wrapped in his arms but she settled for squeezing his hands instead, uncertain if his news was good or not.

"Professor Young has decided to mentor me for my Masters."

"What! Really! That's amazing. How on earth–"

"She's so excited about the fuel's potential that she spoke to the governing board on my behalf and convinced them to let me stay, that I'd be a model student, and she vouched for me."

"Oh my God! Congratulations!" Beth pulled him tight to wrap him in a hug just as fierce as one of Jamie's, but he shifted and tilted his head down catching her lips and igniting the blood in her veins. She gave a little gasp for air before his tongue slipped between her smile and they truly melted into each other for the first time since the Boiler Room.

# ABOUT THE AUTHOR

Growing up in Ontario, Canada, M.J. was the only child of a single mom. M.J.'s passion for the arts ignited at a young age as she wrote adventure stories and read them aloud to close family and friends. The dramatic arts became a focus in high school as an aid to understanding character motivation in her writing. Majoring in Theatre Production at York University, with a minor in English, she went on to teach in both the elementary and high school divisions.

M.J. currently lives with her husband and young son. She keeps busy these days with her emerging authors' website Infinite Pathways, attending book fairs, and conferences as well as holding writing workshops and helping run the WCYR – Writers' Community of York Region.

Connect with M.J. online:

Author Website – www.mjmoores.com

Facebook – www.facebook.com/AuthorMJMoores

Twitter – www.twitter.com/AuthorMJMoores